the day he disappeared

BOOKS BY CATHERINE MILLER

99 Days With You
The Day that Changed Everything
The Missing Piece
The Girl Who Couldn't Leave
The Crash
A Life Lived Beautifully
The Day I Lost Her

All That is Left of Us
Waiting for You

Christmas at the Gin Shack
The Gin Shack on the Beach

CATHERINE MILLER

the day he disappeared

bookouture

Published by Bookouture in 2024

An imprint of Storyfire Ltd.
Carmelite House
50 Victoria Embankment
London EC4Y 0DZ

www.bookouture.com

Storyfire Ltd's authorised representative in the EEA is Hachette Ireland
8 Castlecourt Centre
Castleknock Road
Castleknock
Dublin 15 D15 YF6A
Ireland

ISBN: 978-1-83525-854-5
eBook ISBN: 978-1-83525-853-8

To Eden, my youngest by twenty-seven minutes and our perfect package.

PROLOGUE

What are the things that matter on the day you die?

Is it the place you're in? Or the loved ones that surround you?

I like to think that it's the number of times I've let the wind hit my face and appreciated the fact that I've got my feet firmly planted in the sand.

I like to think it's the number of times I've said, 'I love you' to you each morning in bed and truly meant it.

I like to think it's a culmination of the times we've laughed so loud it's hit the clouds and the sound of your laughter has filled the air.

It's the things that are hard to mark on a map. The things that are difficult to measure because they should be part of every day. The things you can't necessarily grasp in the palm of your hand.

I think those are the things that matter. The love you leave behind. The memories that will last beyond your final breath. The sound of your happiness filling the air that somehow remains there once it is over.

Whatever day it happens, it's the other parts that I hope you remember.

I just wish my life didn't have to leave you so soon...

CHAPTER ONE

KATE

Kate's favourite days with her brother, Matthew, were the ones when he had played a stupid prank on her and they both ended up laughing so much it hurt. Like the time he'd purchased one hundred tiny ducks and hidden them all over the house, much to their parents' frustration.

The worst days with her brother were when he coughed so much his lips turned blue. Those days had filled the calendar over the past two months.

Matthew was currently an inpatient, which he often was for more than half the year. Her younger brother had been diagnosed with cystic fibrosis as a boy and now he was in his mid-twenties, the battles with chest infections seemed to be getting harder on him. What would just be a common cold for most had become a month-long admission for him and, in a cruel twist, he was allergic to the more modern drugs designed to help.

Kate had been helping with her brother's care all her adult life. Most days she would carry out his physiotherapy treatment for him. At a point when most siblings would be drifting apart as they entered their adult life, Kate and Matthew saw each other most days. Kate had stayed at home and combined her nursing degree with continuing to help care for Matthew. And a decade on, although she now shared a house with some nursing colleagues, making regular trips to see Matthew to carry out his treatment was part of her daily timetable. In fact, she was on a zero-hours contract at the hospital so she could be on call for her brother whenever he needed her.

But right now, they were locked in a rare argument.

'You should go! Life's too short to not enjoy yourself every now and then,' Matthew reassured her.

'But…?' Kate squirmed in her seat. She didn't like arguing with her brother, especially when she knew he had a point. But she couldn't remember the last time she had done something just for *her*.

'But nothing, Kate. I'm *okay* at the moment. You have to take the opportunity while you can. I *insist*.'

Kate pondered for a moment, staring at her brother. They shared distinctive red hair and deep-blue eyes and had, in the past, been mistaken for twins.

She glanced around the hospital room and wondered when their version of 'okay' had become so warped. *Okay* would see him at home. *Okay* would see him off oxygen. *Okay* wouldn't involve all the help he was getting just to be able to breathe.

'Lauren won't mind if I miss her hen weekend,' Kate murmured anxiously. 'She already knows there's a possibility I won't be able to come. Especially when it's so far away.'

'I'm not letting you miss out on another occasion because of me. You've done far too much of that over the years. You should take advantage of the fact you can go. That's the possibility you need to fulfil.'

Kate didn't reply. She knew it was pointless when her brother was being insistent over something. If he was well enough to argue, she should probably listen. But there was the part of her that found it hard not to worry. He was in hospital, after all. She didn't want him to know about the concerns she always carried. She didn't want to think of the extra work her parents would have to do with her gone. It was two nights. A weekend in Southfern, a coastal town in Devon. A break from being on the outskirts of London. She could allow herself that, couldn't she?

'You know Mum and Dad will be here looking after me,' Matthew added to his argument, the point he was making intertwining with her thoughts.

'Fine, I'll go!' she conceded. She knew it had been too long since she last let her hair down.

'Good. You need to enjoy yourself. Drink something multi-coloured on my behalf.'

Having her brother's blessing didn't help remove her guilt. And she had a terrible feeling it wasn't going to work out in the way she'd want it to. But, then again, she always felt like that. She needed to snap out of always being so negative.

The problem was that the fear didn't go away. Not as she packed. Not as she made her way to the train station to meet the others. Not even at their shrieks of delight at seeing her arrive on the platform.

There was a reason she didn't tend to go too far for any length of time. It was the love and concern she had for her brother.

She just had to hope she wouldn't regret her decision.

CHAPTER TWO
KATE

The giant inflated penis required three of them to carry it. Freya had purchased it as a joke, not expecting Lauren – the bride to be – to become quite so attached to it, insisting they took it with them to every bar they went to.

Kate was part of the carrying crew and she'd drunk enough to not care too much about any of the strange looks they were receiving. This hen do was probably the biggest event to have occurred this week in Southfern, a usually sleepy Devon town, and it was certainly the most phallic.

Freya and Lauren had been Kate's work colleagues since she'd qualified as a nurse. They all worked on D4, a respiratory-specialist ward, together, and were close friends as well. The rest of the group were Lauren's relatives, and Kate was already too drunk to remember everyone's names. But there was definitely a future mother-in-law here so Kate was trying to be on her best behaviour. She was so glad to have made it to this weekend.

'Time to swap!' Lauren yelled from the front.

Kate's arms were relieved. It wasn't heavy, it was just the bulk of the thing making it awkward to carry. Lauren's mum took over her spot and Kate swung her arms about as if she'd just been in the gym and needed a post-workout stretch.

'Do you know where we're going?' Kate asked Lauren, who was still at the front, unwilling to let go of her prize.

'To the nearest drinking establishment!' her friend replied with a grin.

'Shall I check which way we need to go on my phone?'

'If you could.'

As they'd been to three pubs already, Kate was pretty certain they might have pub crawled their way through the small town in record time. When she finally managed to bring up Google Maps, she discovered there was one other place, but in the opposite direction.

'It looks like there's an Italian restaurant with a bar. We should be able to get a drink there.'

'Let the helmet lead the way!' Lauren said with the joyous energy of someone due to zealously puke in approximately two hours' time. Possibly sooner.

'That's the wrong way!' Kate said as Lauren started to march off in the same direction.

'About turn, everyone. Let's follow Kate the satnav.'

Kate never thought she'd be leading a group of women and their prized giant penis, but she was very thankful to be here with them. She allowed navigating to take over any of the grumbling concerns about Matthew that she hadn't been able to completely silence. The ones reminding her that her brother's lips still had that bluish hue that never allowed her to fully relax.

The Italian restaurant had a narrow doorway, not wide enough for their current load.

'What are we going to do?' Lauren wailed, not coherent enough to work it out.

'That's nothing a touch of flaccidity can't fix,' Lauren's mum, Octavia, called out.

'*Mother!*' Lauren yelled from the front.

'Well, if you will *insist* on dragging a giant cock around you need to know how to handle it. Good thing you invited a woman of experience along. It's a skill to know how to deflate them as much as anything else.'

They all watched as Octavia unplugged the stopper and a slow whistle of air dispersed like a prolonged fart. The six women immediately fell into a fit of laughter that was hard to control. This only increased when a handsome waiter came out to see if there was anything that he'd be able to help with.

'Could you take this in for me, please?' Octavia asked. 'I don't think these women are capable at this point.'

Kate thought he might refuse, but he did so happily under Octavia's supervision. It turned out the restaurant was quiet and having six women turn up at once would be the biggest rush they'd get that evening. Rather than sitting at the bar, they gathered round a large circular table and ordered wine along with pizza and garlic bread. They needed as much starch as possible to help mop up the alcohol consumption.

When the food was delivered to the table, Kate found she was laughing to herself.

'What's so funny?' Lauren asked, shoving a large piece of garlic bread into her mouth.

Kate started laughing again. The type of laughter that made it hard to breathe. The kind of laughter that she'd forgotten she was capable of. It reached every part of her body and reminded her why not only had she wanted to come here, but why she'd *needed* to. It took her four attempts to tell them what had set her off.

'Your mum saying... *flaccidity*. I don't think I've ever heard it used in a sentence before. I've only ever seen it in textbooks.'

At that they all fell into another round of laughter, Kate finding it hard to regain her composure. If they hadn't lost it already, they completely did at the point the giant inflatable folded at the bar, as if it was resigning itself to their terrible hen-party induced sense of humour.

Her phone ringing brought Kate to her senses, especially when she saw the caller ID. It was her parents. It was as if someone had thrown ice over her, the change in her mood was like going from the sauna to a freezing cold bath.

Kate's parents shared a phone, which meant she never knew whether she was going to get her mum or dad on the end of the call, but either way she knew it would be bad news. They'd agreed that unless anything worrying happened with Matthew they wouldn't call. They'd both been part of the conversation when that agreement had been made, so it wasn't like she had the hope that the message hadn't been passed on as sometimes happened between the pair of them.

'Hello?' Kate answered, moving away from the table of giggling hens, not worrying if she knocked anything over on her way outside.

'Kate, is that you?' her mum, Alice, asked from the other end.

'Yes, can you hear me? I've just moved outside the restaurant. Is everything okay?'

The cold air felt like a slap, startling her closer to sober.

'Matthew's taken a turn for the worse, love. They've had to put him on non-invasive ventilation and...'

There was a pause that felt darker than the night sky because it was a gap that didn't hold any stars. That pause was a cavern where no hope was stored.

'Is he...? Does he...?' Kate was too afraid to finish the sentences, too scared of what the answer would be.

'He didn't want me to call, darling, but the doctors have said they're not sure how much longer he's got left and...'

The noise of quiet sobbing came from the other end of the phone and Kate knew her mum couldn't say any more. No one wanted to face what they were facing. And how typical for her to justify a weekend away only for things to get worse. She should have trusted her instincts and never left in the first place.

'I'm leaving now. I'll catch the next train. I'll be there as soon as I can.'

There was the continued noise of her mother trying to control her tears coming from the other end. A sound that made it all too real. Her mum rarely cried.

'And, Mum, thank you for calling. I know Matthew can be stubborn about getting his own way, but if the time has come, you know I'd never forgive myself if I wasn't there.'

Kate held her phone to her chest for a moment after the call ended. The fragility of this life was almost too much to bear at times. They'd known they were drawing ever closer to this point, but why did it have to come when they weren't ready?

'Is everything okay?' It was Lauren, also looking far more sober than she had only a few minutes before.

'It's Matthew.'

Lauren gave a knowing nod. All of her friends here knew about her brother. He might not be a patient on their ward, but they always asked after him. And everyone knew that a phone call this late at night was never going to be good news. 'Is he...?'

'They've put him on non-invasive ventilation. It's only a matter of time.'

'Then we need to get you back to him as soon as possible.'

Lauren shot back into the restaurant as if she hadn't touched a drop of alcohol and got the party all assembled, ready to return to their Airbnb.

Kate had never been more grateful for her friends. There were no murmurs about ruining the hen do. Their only concern was getting her back in time. It had always been a risk that this would happen, but in terms of calculations it had seemed like it was a safe time to be away. As safe as it ever would be.

'What about this?' the waiter shouted at them as they

tottered off in a hurry. The man that had welcomed them into the restaurant was standing waving the partly deflated cock.

'I'll take it! Thank you for everything,' Lauren said, managing to run back for it as if she wasn't wearing heels.

'Don't blow it up again. We don't want that thing slowing us down,' Octavia advised.

'We're not blowing it up. Kate's going to take it home. Matthew *insisted* that she come, and so I think she should take the prop with her so he'll know how much fun we've had when you see him, eh? Now let's get you back to his bedside,' Lauren said.

'Thank you,' Kate whispered, not able to take a big enough lungful of air to add volume to her words.

And from that point, every second was a bridge. Every logistical issue was an ocean. They were all things getting in the way of Kate returning to be by her brother's side. She should never have come here. Because it was too far. There were too many miles to overcome and she'd never been more afraid that she wouldn't be able to navigate her way back to his side.

What if she didn't make it in time?

CHAPTER THREE

KATE

The wind was starting to blow a gale as they made their way back. It had gone from a mild evening to a storm gathering. Kate's long red hair was flying in all directions and when they got near to the beach, she had to shield her face from the sand.

If it wasn't one thing going wrong, it was another and once they were back at the Airbnb, Kate was glad to have a moment alone to weep silently as she gathered her things. Between them they researched every possible way of transporting Kate back to her brother. It would be just over three and a half hours to drive from Southfern to Littleton-on-Thames, but they didn't have a car between them and, even if that was an option, none of them were sober enough to drive. No taxi services were available at that time of night from the village. Nobody owned a helicopter, either.

In the end, the only feasible solution was for Kate to get the earliest train possible in the morning. In theory it gave Kate a couple of hours to sleep, but, of course, that wasn't possible with how she was feeling. Instead, she drank water to sober herself up some more, pacing while she did. The hours and minutes dragged by.

During that time, she tried to recall happier moments. She thought about trips to the park when they'd been children before their lives had revolved around hospital visits. She thought about the tiny plastic ducks and how once they'd all been gathered, the pair of them would plant them around their parents' house once more. She thought about the times when the sun had been shining enough for them to enjoy a drink together in the local beer garden.

Those were the memories she attempted to wade in, not the knowledge that the wait she was enduring might be the time in which she missed her beloved brother's final moments. The fleeting time was making her regret the decision to come here all over again.

Freya and Lauren both got up to say goodbye. Given it was five thirty in the morning, the gesture was appreciated.

'Let us know what happens. We'll head back early as well if you need us to,' Lauren offered.

'No, you enjoy the last night. Get yourselves to the beach once you've got some more sleep.' Despite what Kate was facing, she didn't want it to ruin Lauren's hen weekend. She didn't want this to cast a shadow.

Thankfully, after waving goodbye to her friends, the train station wasn't far, and she managed to walk there in less than ten minutes. She'd never been such a dishevelled mess. The curls she'd added to her red hair yesterday were now flat and her pale skin was covered in streaks from her waterproof mascara having massively failed. She'd not even changed out of her miniskirt. She had at least wrapped herself in a jumper to protect herself from the wind and switched her heels for trainers. Over the past few hours, a storm had been and gone, only adding to her sense of turmoil.

As she walked quickly, she cursed herself again for having gone away in the first place. This had always been a risk. Sometimes it wasn't always possible to avoid the cracks in the pavement and this felt like one of those occasions, only today she'd fallen down and was never going to get out.

When she arrived on the platform, no one else was there. It was far too early for anyone to be up given it was the weekend. Unable to settle, she paced, glancing at the digital numbers on the information board every time she passed it, willing the minutes to go quicker. Time seemed to have slowed down and she desperately wanted to magic herself to her brother's bedside.

By the time the train arrived, a couple of other passengers had gathered. Kate didn't pay much attention to the solitary male that joined her in the same carriage, only noted that he was giving her space. The state she was in probably gave out signals that told him that was what she needed. She'd never been so relieved to take a seat and know that she was heading in the right direction. That needed to be the case because who knew when the time would arrive for her to say goodbye.

She'd heard her phone ping with a message more than once but she wasn't brave enough to look. If it was too late, she didn't want to know. She'd be broken if that was the case. She just had to hold onto the hope that those seconds hadn't ticked away already.

Because she had an awful feeling that she might already be too late.

CHAPTER FOUR

THEO

Theo wasn't in the habit of being up this early, but he'd been working away from the office for a change. It was the evening meal with his clients that made him decide he should get the first morning train, rather than leave so late last night.

It wasn't often he worked beyond the outskirts of London where the office was based in Littleton-on-Thames, so it made a nice change to be elsewhere. That hadn't stopped the desire to be back home to carry on with his usual weekend routine. Leaving early in the morning meant he'd still have time to go and shop for his grandparents and then take his nephew, George, out for a few hours this afternoon, like he did every Saturday.

But those thoughts of home didn't stop him from noticing the woman on the platform at Southfern station as soon as he arrived. It was hard not to when her red hair seemed to be fighting the wind from the tail end of the storm. That and the fact she was clinging to what appeared to be a wilted inflatable penis. He found the combination was beautifully hypnotic and, when he caught her eye, he smiled, but it wasn't returned. Instead, she looked away, probably hoping he hadn't noticed her reddened eyes. There was something about her that made him want to make sure she was okay because, for some reason, he already sensed she was in need of help.

Theo swiftly reminded himself there weren't too many British commuters that enjoyed communicating with other people, especially if they were upset. Theo guessed she'd had a heavy night so completely understood why she might not want to interact right now. He put some distance between them, so she knew not to be concerned, but when the two-carriage train arrived, he found himself getting onto the same one as her. Her hair continued to billow, mesmerising him until they were out of the wind.

Theo chose a seat where it was easy to set his laptop up. Even though it was early on a Saturday morning, he always liked to use travel time to catch up, and he might as well get cracking while the details the client wanted changing were fresh in his memory. Although he had his notes to refer to, he knew most of the points that would need altering without referring to them.

He co-owned an architectural firm with his best friend, Owen, and their books were full. They'd taken on a few more projects outside their geographical area this year and it was proving to be a good move in terms of widening their portfolio. This current project was one he'd already worked on. They'd created pods for a glamping retreat, and now they were looking to expand further. They wanted to create more accommodation in a barn and a natural swimming pool in keeping with their eco-retreat credentials. He'd started creating the new plans on his laptop, knowing they'd require planning permission and as that sometimes took a while it was worth cracking on with.

It was when he was close to completing the first graphics for his clients that the Tannoy crackled into life.

'We'll be stopping ahead of the next station due to a tree on the line. I'll give you a further update as soon as I know anything further.'

Normally a collective groan would ring out at such news, but it was only Theo and the woman in this carriage and her response was to cry out... loudly.

'*Noooo!*' she wailed.

Saving the work he'd done, Theo glanced over to her seat to see if she was okay. She was holding her head in her hands and had started to sob. Clearly she wasn't alright, but that didn't help him know what to do.

He thought about his sister, Anita, and what she'd want to happen in this situation. The problem was his sister would probably give a different answer depending on the position of the moon, the stage of her menstrual cycle, or whether she'd eaten yet. Sometimes she'd openly welcome his concern, other times it would make her wail all the harder. The stranger reminded him of his sister. She must be a similar age, and her current state made him want to help. No one should go through tough times alone.

Theo realised he couldn't use any of his previous experience to help make a decision. He was going to have to decide on what he knew about his fellow passenger, which wasn't much. Her attire, the inflatable and the sash hanging from her bag provided a big clue, she must be coming from a hen party. The streaks he'd spotted down her cheeks indicated she was upset before the announcement, but that news had upset her further.

He knew very little else.

She might have found something out and was ready to call her wedding off. She might be an uninvited wedding guest as the result of something that had happened.

He was going to have to ask. Even then, he'd only know if she wanted to tell him. But he needed to offer his help, because her cries reminded him of the loss his family had suffered when his father had died.

Having hesitated for far too long already, Theo left his seat and found the pack of tissues he always had on him, normally reserved for his nephew.

'Would you like some tissues?' Theo held them outstretched as if they were some kind of sign for *I come in peace*.

The woman froze and only offered a side eye to assess what was happening, her beautiful red hair cascading over her face.

'I just wanted to make sure you're okay?'

She shook her head, more tears escaping as she did so.

He wasn't sure what to say. He'd hate it if his sister were in a similar state. Before he managed to form a comforting sentence, the noise of the Tannoy drowned out all other conversation.

'I've had an update and I'm afraid to say we're going to be stuck here until the tree has been safely removed. A specialist team is on their way, and I'll update you again when I have any more information. In the meantime, I'm in carriage two if anyone has any questions.' As there were only two carriages, it meant he was in the one next to them.

Theo wasn't entirely sure what to do. He didn't want to leave her, and he knew it would be irresponsible to just return to his laptop. His arm was still outstretched with the tissues he was offering.

She glanced at him properly for the first time and their eyes locked. Hers shone with a deep-blue colour as if they'd been painted by the ocean, and Theo couldn't look away. It was a moment of communication without words. Looking into her deep-blue eyes, Theo sensed she wanted him to stay until she was ready to talk and, after a moment or two, she accepted the tissues and managed to gain some composure.

'I'm okay, honestly. I'm sorry for disrupting your work.' She glanced to where his abandoned laptop remained.

Theo was still caught up in the ocean of her eyes. For some reason, he had a sudden urge to make sure neither of them drowned. And he had a strange feeling that he was here to make sure she was okay for a reason. He just needed to work out what that reason was.

'Work can wait. Do you want to talk about what's upsetting you?'

If there had been a wrong thing to say, that was probably it as her composure was lost again for another few minutes, a tissue sacrificed in the meantime.

'We don't have to talk if that's too much. I have tea in a flask if you want a cup, would that help?' Theo's nan had taught him to always travel with a hot flask because there were always occasions when it would come in handy. This definitely classed as one of those.

The woman shook her head. 'Oh God, I'm sorry to be so dramatic... it's just...' She dried her face of tears with another tissue as she attempted to speak. 'My brother is dying. Might already be...'

She broke off into tears again and now he knew why, it wasn't surprising. No one would want to be stuck on a train with that going on.

'I take it you're on your way to see him?'

She nodded. 'Yes, he's in West Middlesex Hospital.'

At those words, Theo knew that he'd be able to help this woman. And, more than that, he knew that he *wanted* to help her. Wanted to do anything at all to stop the tears flowing from those beautiful eyes.

'That's not far from where I work. My car is parked at the station, so I can give you a lift once we get there. In the meantime, I'll go and speak to the train guard.'

'I just want to get to my brother. Whatever it takes...'

'Let me ask the guard what the situation is.'

Now Theo knew why she was so upset, he was going to do everything in his power to help. No wonder she'd reminded him of when his sister had been so distressed when they'd lost their father. The parallels were too close for comfort as those memories threatened to overwhelm him.

Theo focussed on pressing the button that released the carriage doors. There was only one other passenger in this section, so there was no queue to worry about. The guard informed him they wouldn't be able to move as there was another train in one direction and the tree in the other. The tree surgeons were doing their best and he hoped to have another update within the next half hour.

It was not much news to return with. He sensed that half hour might make all the difference, only in the wrong way. Some words turned in his head that were something close to a prayer.

Theo relayed the little he'd learned to the woman, who seemed more composed compared to when he'd left her.

'Can I change my mind about that cup of tea?' she asked, before he sat down.

'Of course. Let me go and get my things.' Moving over to where he'd been sitting, Theo closed his laptop down and put it away, before carrying all his belongings to the section of seats where she was.

'I'm Theo, by the way.' He'd normally stretch out his arm and offer his hand, but he hadn't finished putting his laptop away.

'I'm Kate. Thank you for the tissues and tea, Theo.'

'Nice to meet you, Kate. I just wish it was under a better set of circumstances for you. I hope you like milk with your tea? I've already added some.' Theo poured from the tartan-printed Thermos into the metal lid.

'That's how I normally take it – thanks.' Kate took the proffered cup and drank it as if she had a great thirst.

Theo had met a lot of people in his lifetime, but somehow none of them had seemed as important as this woman. Whether it was because of the urgency of her current predicament, and the fact he would be able to help, or because he'd felt a connection he wasn't able to explain, it was hard to tell. But whatever he would end up putting it down to, he knew that it would last beyond this train journey.

Even if it was only so he'd get her where she needed to be, he knew it mattered.

CHAPTER FIVE

KATE

Even though this was the worst day of Kate's life, Theo – with his tartan flask and pale-yellow checked trousers that somehow matched his hair – was managing to distract her enough for the pain to bubble under the surface, rather than boil over.

If it had been any other set of circumstances, she'd have considered this winning at a game of bingo. After all, he was the most attractive man she'd met in some time, and he was helping her. But today, nothing could pull her thoughts from her brother. Instead, she and Theo had talked about all their favourite things so far.

Colours – Him: red. Her: yellow.

Foods – Him: curry. Her: steak pie from the hospital canteen.

Places to visit – Him: castles. Her: beaches.

Music – Him: classical. Her: K-pop.

They'd discovered, as random luck would have it, that they were from the same area – Littleton-on-Thames – and yet had never landed up in the same place until now. The thing they hadn't talked about was her brother. She knew if they did, she'd soon revert to the blubbering mess Theo had found her in. His company was providing the distraction she needed to stop her from trying to claw her way out to scramble along the track and find another method of transport. She'd charter a helicopter if she had the means to. Anything to ensure she got to say goodbye...

She'd always known it was going to happen. She was four years older than Matthew and still had a vague memory of when her mum and dad had sat her down to explain they'd been told by the doctors why her brother was so prone to chest infections. They'd carried out some tests and discovered he had cystic fibrosis. They'd explained how he was going to need their help to keep him healthy.

At the time she'd not fully comprehended what that meant, but as soon as she'd been old enough to, she'd started helping with his chest physio. What sister wouldn't when it meant being able to thump her brother with her parents' permission? Although thumping wasn't exactly an accurate description. Not when the proper term was percussion. And rather than using a balled fist it was a cupped hand, but that didn't mean she hadn't got in the occasional rib dig over the years. Matthew was her brother, after all.

Since she was in her teens, Kate had done at least one of his chest physio sessions most days. It was a way of keeping his lungs as clear as possible and it was the reason they'd always been close as siblings. There probably weren't many brothers and sisters that willingly spent a concentrated period of time together each day well into adulthood.

But it had never stopped Kate from doing what she wanted. She'd managed to train as a nurse at the local university and the evenings she couldn't cover, her parents always would. They'd been a tight-knit family as a result, always making sure they were there to help out. In more recent years, the hospital admissions had become more frequent and the chances of his eligibility for a lung transplant had narrowed to zero. They'd known losing Matthew was on the cards, it had been edging ever closer. She'd been there nearly every day for him. She'd not been away for a weekend for ages. This *couldn't* be the time that he slipped away from her.

'If you could travel to any country right now, where would you go?' Kate asked, realising her thoughts were moving dangerously close to the point where she would be crying again. She felt the sudden urge to hold Theo's hand as if it would anchor her to a happier place. She wasn't sure where that notion had come from and reminded herself that she didn't want to scare him off. Not before getting a lift.

'Are there any limits to this?'

Kate shrugged. 'Nope, no limits.'

'In that case, we're going to the moon. I've always wanted to be able to fly. Ever since I was a lad, the best superpower for me was always the ability to fly. As we can't do that without sitting in a plane on earth, I reckon the best place to head would be the moon. That way I can experience weightlessness which must be as close to flying as it gets. What about you?'

It didn't take any thinking time for Kate to come up with her answer. 'Iceland, although I'd need to get a passport. I've never been abroad.'

'Haven't you?' There was a note of surprise in his voice.

'Nope. I know most people in their twenties have, but I've always been looking after my brother.'

For a second, Kate imagined travelling there with Theo. It was a daydream she wasn't able to fully indulge in with her present state of mind.

Suddenly, the loudspeaker crackled into life, bringing her back to the nightmare and she clasped her hands almost in prayer. It had to be better news this time.

'I'm pleased to report the obstruction has been moved off the track, so we'll be moving again shortly. We'll be travelling at a slower speed than usual while we pass through that area as

THE DAY HE DISAPPEARED   25

there's still some work in progress. This will cause a short delay to travel times, but we're on our way.'

Kate should be delighted at such an announcement, but the added knowledge that the service would run slower than usual really wasn't helping.

'I hope it doesn't take us too long to get there.'

'I just hope we get there in time for you.'

So did Kate.

Because by this point her parents had sent several messages, and she still wasn't brave enough to read them.

CHAPTER SIX

THEO

Theo had never driven over the speed limit in his life. He was trying not to now, but he was keeping the needle as close to the limits of each road as possible. He was doing it in the hope he was able to save Kate some heartache. He hadn't been able to do that for himself and his sister when their dad had suffered a second heart attack. They hadn't managed to be there by his side, so it felt important to get Kate to her brother's bedside as soon as possible.

Any minute now Kate's brother might take his last breath and, even though he hadn't known this woman when he'd woken up this morning, it had become the most important car journey of his life. Being in the driving seat had never carried such an important function and he willed every mile to disappear. For every piece of traffic to move out of the way. For there to be clear roads all the way to the hospital.

Sadly, there was the odd car, or set of traffic lights, that got in the way and even though he felt like swearing obscenities, he kept that sealed as he didn't want to add to the worried expression on Kate's face.

They barely spoke on the journey. He'd managed to distract

her with asking about her favourite things on the train. He didn't feel like he could distract her with anything frivolous for the rest of the drive, especially given his concentration was focussed on making sure he got her there safely and as quickly as possible.

'Head towards the eye department entrance. It's the quickest route in from there,' Kate instructed.

Seeing signs for the hospital brought both relief and added tension. Theo felt the atmosphere change in the car without either of them saying anything.

'Will do,' he said in as reassuring a voice as possible.

There were three more roads to navigate that involved several sets of traffic lights, a hill and a mini roundabout. He knew the route well after bringing his grandad to all his eye appointments, so he didn't need to ask for directions.

'I really hope we've made it in time,' he said, but the words came out empty.

Two roads to go.

Theo sped across the mini roundabout without slowing down as much as he usually would, but he'd checked enough to make sure it was safe.

One road to go.

'You've done everything you can to get here as soon as possible.' Theo wasn't sure why he was saying anything. It certainly wasn't lessening any tension. Knowing that, he reached over and gave Kate's hand a quick squeeze. A perhaps too intimate move for the length of time he'd known her, but given the circumstances a touch of reassurance seemed necessary.

No roads to go.

Theo pulled into the hospital and headed towards the drop-off space near the entrance to the eye unit.

Kate was undoing her seat belt and started to open the passenger door before he had the handbrake on.

Turning off the engine and ensuring the gears were in

neutral, Theo flung himself out of the car as fast as possible and went to give Kate a hand. She already had her backpack on and her deflated cushion that used to be a hen do prop.

'Do you need any help?'

'No, I'm okay. But thank you, for everything. I need to go.' Kate kissed him briefly on the cheek.

Theo found himself holding that patch on his face and watching her disappear as she whizzed into the entrance. It was as if an enigma had come into his life and just as quickly had disappeared out of it.

Theo remained frozen for some time. He wanted to follow her. He wanted to know the conclusion to this story. He felt bereft now she was gone as if she'd taken a part of him with her. He wanted to know whether they'd made it in time. But it would be too intrusive to follow just to satisfy his curiosity.

A car beeped its horn, and that sound was what he needed to unlock himself. He might have remained on the spot for evermore otherwise, hoping to see Kate again. Hoping that he might learn the end of this story.

'Sorry!' he said to the waiting driver and waved his hand.

Theo clambered into his car, knocking his knee hard as he did so. Pulling away he realised he needed to head to his grandparents' to make a start on their shopping. He was running later than he'd planned with the train delay and the diversion to the hospital. But somehow, it felt too soon to just return to his usual routine.

Despite knowing that he was going to be late, Theo pulled into the side of the road at the soonest opportunity. He did it so he could rub his knee, but also so he had a moment to allow his body to calm down. The adrenaline had been pumping through him on the way here and it wasn't even close to starting to ebb away.

'Sometimes we don't get to find out how the story ends,' he

said out loud to himself. 'And sometimes we have to write the ending ourselves.'

They were the words of wisdom his mother had offered when his dad had passed away. The event this reminded him of. He'd only been fourteen at the time and it felt as if the walls of his life had crumbled and fallen around him. But those sentences had always given him comfort. It was true, sometimes it wasn't possible to know how the story ends.

He wasn't sure why, but he really hoped he would see Kate again. He felt a sense of loss that was nothing to do with lost fathers or brothers.

The loss was to do with the lingering trace of a kiss on his cheek. The sense of a blossom attempting to bloom against a storm.

CHAPTER SEVEN

KATE

Navigating the corridors felt as if it was a game of The Floor is Lava. As Kate not only worked here, but spent many hours by her brother's side, she knew the route like the back of her hand. But numerous obstacles had been added and the people traffic seemed to be at a peak. It felt like she was hopping from one foot to another, and the usual straight paths were all ones she was having to curve along.

She'd been expecting the worst the entire time she'd been travelling home, right up until she'd called her parents to ask where to head. Their answer was a sign that the messages she'd ignored hadn't held the news that she'd feared.

She could feel her heartbeat in her throat by the time she arrived at the high-dependency unit where he was now being looked after. The fact he was only on the high-dependency unit now, Kate knew was a good sign. But it wouldn't be long before they'd take him back to the isolation unit where he was normally admitted.

'Bloody hell, Matthew! Can you make sure you never do that to me again?' Kate practically shouted at her brother, who was sitting up, a crooked smile forming on seeing her. What she'd been imagining and what she was being presented with were two worlds apart.

The relief at seeing him upright and compos mentis was untold. Especially when Kate had feared the worst, but there were telltale signs of how ill he was. His skin was grey and he'd lost some weight and there were drips that hadn't been there and pinpricks that told her they'd put additional lines in.

Kate perhaps knew more about the outward signs because of her job, but even without that she was able to see how unwell he still was. That they were only millimetres away now.

'The hens made me bring you a present back,' Kate said, realising she'd been staring for too long, analysing all the outward signs as if she were Sherlock Holmes.

'That's.' Inhale. Exhale. 'Good.' Inhale. Exhale. 'Of them.'

Kate did her best to focus on what he was saying rather than what his respiratory rate was doing. Another sign that his body was struggling. Full sentences had taken a holiday.

'You might not say that when you see what it is.'

Kate was still holding the deflated penis. She'd carried it for so long it felt like an arch nemesis. But after being gifted it to give him she'd felt as if it was almost a lucky charm. If she could get it to him, all would be well.

And it was. Because he was *alive*.

She knew that wouldn't be the case next time. She knew they were running on limited time. Having run a fine line, she knew she wouldn't take any more trips away. She was going to remain nearby, because their luck, whatever there was of it, was due to run out.

Matthew unfolded some of the plastic, which squeaked as the form of two balls flopped out.

'It's not...?' their mum, Alice, squeaked.

'I've come directly from a hen party, so it definitely *is*.' Kate raised her eyebrow at her mum. She didn't need to look quite so shocked over the phallic prop.

'Well, sis.' In. Out. 'I'll let you blow it up.' Matthew paused for another second, making sure he didn't get too breathless. 'If I do. It might finish me off.'

'You are not blowing that up in here!' Alice declared, acting more prim and proper than ever before, the stress of the past few hours taking her nerves to the edge.

'She's right.' Matthew's lips broke into a slow grin. 'I'm too ill for a blow job.'

'*Matthew!*'

And just as her brother had expected, it made Kate laugh so hard she snorted as their mother despaired at the pair of them. She felt like she was a pan boiling over: the sudden release of tension allowing tears to roll for reasons she hadn't expected. Her brother was still alive and making terrible jokes that were offending their mother! It was a *joy* to see her mother's indignation caused by her brother who less then twelve hours before had been close to death.

'Shall I volunteer myself, seeing as Kate isn't going to be able to help out?' their dad, Malcolm, offered.

Kate noticed how grey and sunken her dad's eyes were despite his smile, and it told her how tired he must be.

'Malcolm! Don't encourage them!' Alice chastised.

'I think it's allowed on this occasion. It is a gift, and all the hens are nurses from this hospital. We might get kicked out if they *don't* find it installed.' Kate's dad offered a wink in her direction, perhaps realising her histrionics were the result of the most stressful journey of her life. She was an emotional jumble, and her laughter was the result.

'It's going to get in the way! What if it knocks one of his machines?' Alice continued to fail to see the funny side of it.

Kate managed to regain control over her fit of giggles. She knew that her mum wasn't able to laugh in this situation and she understood why. Matthew was edging ever closer to the end. Had very nearly been there.

It might only be another twenty-four hours before things changed for the worse again. They weren't out of the woods because, of course, they never would be.

For the rest of the morning, Matthew returned to being a man only able to concentrate on his next breath and then his next. There were no conversations with him. Only monosyllable words. Yes. No. Thanks.

And similarly, Kate only heard the same blunt sounds when it came to discussions about his care. End. Of. Life. Next time, Matthew didn't want any additional treatment. He only wanted to be kept comfortable.

'Is there anything else you want me to do?' Kate asked, as always keen to make sure her brother was okay before she left.

Matthew's eyes flicked to the inflatable in the corner of the room.

'You know Mum will kill me if I do.'

'You... did... say... *anything*.'

Kate knew what he was up to. Trying to get his sibling in trouble even though he could hardly breathe.

'I'll do it tomorrow. That way you've got something to look forward to.'

'Deal.'

Kate really hoped that was true. That there'd be no more middle of the night emergency calls. But she'd make sure she was close by from this point on. She'd make use of the on-call room on the D4 ward like her ward manager had previously offered.

She wasn't going to risk leaving the hospital again.

CHAPTER EIGHT

THEO

It was Theo's second trip to the hospital that week. The first had been as a last-minute chauffeur in a tragic situation, and thoughts of Kate had been lingering in his mind ever since. He'd frequently wondered if Kate had made it to her brother in time. He'd recalled the first time they'd locked eyes on numerous occasions. He longed to see her fiery-red hair again blowing in the wind. But knowing only her first name and some general details wasn't enough of a link to find out any answers.

This time he was here escorting his nan to her yearly rheumatology appointment. He'd normally go back to his car and work on his laptop, but today he was heading towards the canteen to replenish his fluid levels. That's what he was telling himself. Really it was because he was hoping that the answers to his question about whether they'd arrived in time on Saturday morning might be there. But unless he asked every nurse that he passed – who no doubt wouldn't be able to tell him because of patient confidentiality – how would he ever know?

It was when he sat down with his coffee and a KitKat that he saw her. She was in scrubs, so his brain struggled to believe it was real at first. But he would recognise that red hair and those blue eyes anywhere. He stared in her direction on the other side of the tills to make certain that he didn't scare a stranger.

And she *was* a stranger still, really. Just because they'd spent a few hours in each other's company didn't mean that she'd recognise him either. Her mind had been on other things at the time.

'Kate?' he tried as she left the till.

He said her name loud enough that she'd hear, but not so loud that the whole canteen would be looking at them.

Kate's gaze swung in his direction and a broad smile spread across her face. '*Theo!* What are you doing here?'

Her smile brightened his day so much it was like a firework going off in the sky. Or rather it was as if it had happened inside him. He realised he'd not seen it the other day when her face had been entirely knotted with anxiety. Kate's smile was as beautiful as she was.

'I'm here with my nan. She's got a rheumatology appointment, and they always take a while. I thought I'd come and take a break. How are you? How are things?' Theo didn't know quite how to phrase what he wanted to ask.

'My brother's still with us thankfully. Thank you *so* much for getting me here so quickly the other day. Matthew's still really unwell. I haven't left here since, I don't want to risk a repeat of not being able to get back.'

'I'm glad we managed to get you back after the tree fiasco.'

'It was really kind of you to give me a lift, especially given the state I was in.'

'You don't need to thank me. Anyone with any kind of conscience would have done the same.'

'You and I both know that isn't the world we live in these days.'

'I'm just glad… you know.'

'Me too.'

Theo glanced down at the tray Kate was carrying and registered the fact she'd bought hot food for her lunch. 'Come and sit with me while you eat.' Pulling out a chair, he chastised himself for getting caught up in seeing her, but he'd been revelling in how beautiful she was without mascara down her cheeks. He'd also been so eager to discover what had happened that he'd forgotten etiquette.

'If that's okay?'

'Unless you want your own company, of course. I won't be offended if you want to go and sit by yourself.' There were a lot of lone diners here, all lost in their thoughts by the looks of it. Who knew what any of them were trying to process? There were patients and practitioners alike.

'No, it'll be nice to have company. And I'm definitely in need of hot food so you'll just have to forgive me if I eat like an animal. I haven't had many opportunities to come down here, but Matthew's best friend is visiting, and they suggested I take the opportunity to get a warm meal.'

They sat in silence to begin with, Kate settling into her seat and making a start on her food, while Theo drank his coffee as slowly as possible.

'Do they know how long...?' Theo didn't manage to complete the sentence, but it felt important to ask rather than ignore the elephant in the room.

'Any day really. We don't have long left. I'm just glad it didn't happen whilst I was away. I work on D4 ward part-time and the ward sister has been very kind and is letting me use the on-call room to catch up on sleep without leaving the premises. Fortunately, the rooms come complete with a shower so I don't stink. At least, I don't *think* I do.' Kate abandoned her knife and fork to give her armpit a good sniff.

The gesture made Theo laugh. 'Don't worry... you'd be forgiven if you did stink, given what you're going through.'

'That's good to know.' Kate beamed at him.

Those eyes...

'So what do you do on the ward?' Theo wanted to know more about Kate. The way she looked at him was making him melt inside. She had a quirky element to her that was endearing, and it was lovely to see her far more relaxed than she had been on their first meeting.

'I'm a nurse. I studied part-time over four years to earn my qualification. It's all because of my brother. I think I was quali- fied before I even started out with the amount I've learned by proxy of being his sister. It'll probably be no surprise if I tell you that D4 is a respiratory ward.' She picked up her knife and fork again.

'That's amazing that you've managed to do that alongside helping with your brother.' Theo concentrated on talking to Kate rather than wishing it was his hand that she was holding. He wasn't sure what was coming over him, but now he was in her presence again he was aware of that sense of connection once more. As if there were invisible threads ensuring they were together.

'Now, tell me about *you*. I only know titbits like your favourite colour. I want a full summary while I plough through my food.'

Theo had forgotten about the silly questions he'd come up with as a form of distraction when they'd been waiting on the unmoving train. They'd answered lots of trivia-style options, but neither had gone into the finer details of their lives.

'Okay, well, like you hoping you don't have BO, I'm hopeful this won't bore you. I'm going with the long version so you can eat all your food and chew it for good measure.'

Theo started his speech with a smile, grateful to be in her company once more.

'I've always liked design so when I left school I was deter- mined to become an architect. I hadn't realised how long it would take to be qualified, but I got onto a course at the local university and remained living with my mum to keep the costs low. I then went and worked with several firms, before eventually starting my own company with my best friend, Owen. OT Architects. We're based near the docks in Littleton-on-Thames.'

Kate nodded and finished her mouthful, grinning before speaking. 'I think I've seen the sign for it. Near the cinema, right?'

'Yes, that's the place.' Hearing that she knew about his office only strengthened his conviction there was a connection between them.

Kate was about halfway through her plate of food, and Theo knew he needed to fill the conversation. She was eating as quickly as possible so she'd be able to get back to her brother. There was an openness to the look she gave him, and he knew whatever he told her, he could trust her. He knew he wasn't imagining this link that was forming between them.

'These days my time is spent keeping the business running and my spare time I always spend with my family.'

There was more to that sentence, but given how much Kate was going through at the moment, he didn't know whether to tell her more. When her gaze looked at him expectantly and she gestured for him to continue, he decided he would tell her. It was something he didn't talk about that much, but he didn't want to spend his whole life pretending it hadn't happened. And it felt especially important to share when it was the reason he'd offered to help her in the first place. He knew what it was to deal with the pain she was facing.

'I'm very family focussed because my dad passed away when I was a teenager. It happened really suddenly – a heart attack while he was playing squash. He survived that cardiac event, but less than a day later, when he was in hospital, he had a second catastrophic one. It left a hole in the family that I felt a certain amount of responsibility to fill. That sounds a bit bullishly macho now I'm saying it, but I wanted to make sure my whole family was okay. Surprisingly all these years later, it's not my mum that has needed my help. It's my dad's parents, my grandparents, who lost the person they used to call whenever they needed help with something.

'And my sister, Anita. She got pregnant before she turned twenty and went on to become a single mum to my nephew, George. As his father has never featured in his life, I try and make sure I help my sister out as much as possible. At least one part of my weekend is involved with entertaining George. He would have been the apple of my dad's eye and he's certainly mine.' Theo realised Kate had finished eating and he was still going on. He'd managed to pour out the event that hurt his heart the most and he'd not broken a sweat because he'd found himself able to open up to Kate with ease. 'So, that's my life in a nutshell.'

Kate reached across the table and squeezed his hand. 'I'm sorry to hear about your dad, Theo, but thank you for sharing. It's strangely reassuring to hear about someone getting through the aftermath. I know it's going to be tough.'

Theo wasn't sure sometimes if he *had* got through it, but hearing Kate say that made him realise he must have. Keeping busy was his way of coping. 'I miss my dad a lot, but I think he would have approved of everything we've done since.'

'I'm sure he would.'

With her plate clear, Theo knew she needed to go. She could only allow herself short periods of respite, just in case.

'Can I have your number?' Theo asked. 'I'd like to stay in touch, if that's okay?' He knew she was talking about the aftermath because it was something she was facing. He'd like to be able to offer support if she were ever in need of it. And he couldn't ignore the sense of their connection. As if life knew they'd need each other so had put them in each other's path.

'Of course. I can't believe I didn't share it with you before, but time was of the essence last time I saw you. Shall I put it into your phone?'

Theo passed it over from its resting place on the table. He'd abandoned it as soon as he'd spotted Kate. He'd never offered it up as eagerly as he did in that moment.

Kate spent a moment tapping buttons before passing it back.

'I'll give you a ring and then you'll have mine as well.'

Her phone buzzed from her pocket.

They both gathered everything, and Kate deposited her tray to the right spot. For a moment, they stared at each other whilst at the canteen exit and Theo was aware of how much he wanted to put his hand through her hair, while hugging her close.

'I wish I could do more to help,' Theo said sadly, feeling useless.

'Sharing your story has been help enough. I'll be in touch.'

Kate then gave Theo a quick hug. One that he barely had time to respond to.

It left Theo staring at her wake for the second time that week. He wanted to rewind to the moment she was sniffing her armpits in the middle of the canteen without a care in the world. There was something about that moment he wanted to hold onto and he wasn't sure why. Perhaps because he wanted to hold onto that sense of not caring? Because he knew what she was walking towards wasn't any easier than when he'd left her the other day.

But he knew there was a chance he'd never hear from her again and, for some reason, that thought left him feeling hollow.

CHAPTER NINE

KATE

'What's his name?' Matthew asked.

It was the first full sentence without additional breaths that Kate had heard since she'd returned from the hen do. Her brother was obviously eager to know who'd made her smile again.

'Could be a *she*,' Kate said, not wanting to give anything away. He knew her too well.

'Spill the... beans.'

Kate realised one full sentence didn't mean her brother was better. Not by any measure.

'Okay. It was Theo. He's the guy who gave me a lift from the train station after we'd been stuck on a train because of a tree on the track. I did tell you, but at the time you were too poorly to take note. I've just bumped into him in the canteen.'

'Has he been waiting... all... this time?'

'No! He was waiting for his nan to finish her appointment. But he did ask after you.'

'I hope you... only told him... good things.'

'I told him what an annoying brother you are and he felt so

sorry for me he gave me his number!' So much for not giving anything away.

'Real... ly?'

'Not like that. He's just a nice guy.'

'I want to... meet him.'

'What?'

'You heard! Valiant knight... gives... you his number. I want... to meet him.'

'Why?' Kate must have blushed enough to give away the fact she liked Theo. Which, she realised, she did. They may have only met for a brief period, but he'd already earned a space in her heart in that short time. That didn't mean she wanted to suffer the embarrassment of her brother interrogating him.

'I'm a... dying man. Surely, you... just say yes?'

'You can't play that card. It's illegal.'

'Who says?'

'Hospital policy.'

'Hmm. Not sure... about that.'

Kate nodded her head and hoped that was the end of discussion.

'Because I want... to meet the man... who has... made my sister smile... for the first time... in *months*.'

'It's not the first time in months! I smile all the time.'

'Not... all the way... to your eyes.'

'I *do* smile.' Kate produced the fakest grin she was able to muster.

'Not like that. So... message him. Ask him... to come... say hi.'

'Really?'

'Yes. Don't argue. Do that. Then... it's physio time.'

Kate inwardly screamed. Only her brother could make her do something this awkward. Having realised she really liked Theo, she wasn't sure how she felt about her brother trying to interfere. But she didn't want to continue the argument knowing how much of his breath it was taking up. When Theo had asked for her number she'd imagined contacting him months from now. She'd hoped that at some natural point along the way they'd have got in touch with each other and, if the feeling was mutual, it might have been something to explore later on. She'd not had any plans to contact him yet, even if she had liked him instantly. Not when she had her brother to concentrate on, but here Matthew was, not giving her a choice. Okay, she did have a choice, but she knew she'd like to see Theo again. And it was hard to tell if it was just to appease her brother, or to satisfy her curiosity over how she was feeling about him.

Hi, bit odd, but my brother has asked if he can meet you! Any chance you can pop by? Probably tomorrow would be best. Kate x

She hoped Theo would understand the subtext of the uncertainty of time. It was too impractical to arrange something for today, but if they left it any longer, it might be too late. And despite saying she wasn't entering into meeting a dying man's wish, she knew that was what she was doing. Why else would she have said yes? In other circumstances it might have felt like her brother was setting her up for some juvenile prank. Only they weren't kids anymore and this certainly wasn't any kind of playground.

'I've messaged him,' Kate said, not showing Matthew the actual text for fear he might also work out the subtext or make a big deal over the added kiss.

'Really? I didn't think... you would!' Matthew pulled a face that made Kate want to thump him. It didn't matter the circumstances, some elements of sibling behaviour never changed.

'Can you lie on your side? Your physio is definitely due, if only to shut you up!'

'If I hadn't nudged... you never... would have... messaged. You'll be... thanking me.'

'We'll see.' Kate didn't want to dwell on it ahead of any kind of reply from Theo.

'We will,' Matthew said with far more assurance than Kate would ever be able to muster.

As Matthew lay on his side ready for physio on the lower quadrant of his lung, Kate just thanked her lucky stars that what they were discussing was even a possibility. And even though the thought of their meeting was enough to give her butterflies, it also held an importance she wasn't able to explain.

But as she started the gentle percussion of his ribs that gradually became harder as she went, her brother was too busy clearing phlegm off his chest to be able to answer any questions. Instead, she enjoyed, not for the first time, legally beating her brother up. There had been times when carrying out this task had felt like a responsibility she'd never been prepared for. But over the years, she'd grown accustomed to it. A familiar part of her day that her peers didn't have to endure.

And before long, she wouldn't have to do this, and it was going to leave the biggest gap in her life. On considering that, she paid a little more care and attention to the task in hand. She even extended it to not thinking about it in terms of thumping, but rather, sustaining his life for just a smidgeon longer.

Because they'd reached a point when every single hour counted.

CHAPTER TEN

THEO

Theo had taken a day off work and, not wanting to waste the rest of it, he'd offered to entertain George after school. Despite there having been a bright spell last week, the rain was pouring down this afternoon and for that there was only one solution... indoor soft play.

Theo's sister, Anita, often said she didn't know how he managed to take George to soft play so often without losing his mind. But it was an uncle's blessing. Unlike most of the other parents there, he hadn't been dealing with George 24/7. This was only a concentrated period and he often enjoyed it as much as George did as he joined him on the equipment where it was appropriate – and possible – for adults to venture.

The screeches of delight didn't worry him and even though George was now seven, it hadn't yet become uncool to have his uncle attempting to keep up with him.

'I'm gonna beat you!' George said, ever the competitive one.

'Nah! I've got gravity on my side, buddy.'

George dropped into position at the top of the slide. There were two side by side and they often raced down them.

'Ready, steady...'

'I'm not ready to go yet, bud. Let your uncle make it to the starting position.' Theo eased himself down gently.

He was going to turn thirty next year and he was beginning to feel it. His knee wasn't as cooperative as it had once been and bashing it when getting into his car the other day hadn't helped. Theo figured it was probably down to activities like this that was causing his joints to seize a tad more than they used to. In the future, he wouldn't be able to claim it had been caused by something macho like rugby or football. No, he'd caused any joint problems by taking the slide races with his nephew too seriously.

'Okay, I'm ready,' Theo said once he'd got himself in place.

'*Go!*' George yelled, missing the ready and steady.

Theo had to laugh. He normally gave George a head start, but he guessed it was only fair given he'd said the intro already before Theo had sat down. This time there wasn't a chance gravity would aid him enough to beat his nephew to the bottom.

'Yes, I knew I'd beat you!' George declared as they both came to a juddering stop at the end of the bright plastic slides.

'Ah, you got me this time, George! Want to go again?' Theo hauled himself back onto two feet.

'Yeah!' George yelled and started running up the stairs at a pace Theo was never going to keep up with.

As he trundled up the stairs as quickly as his legs would take him, his watch pinged notifying him of a text message on his phone. He glanced at it briefly with the name Kate immediately increasing his pulse. He hadn't thought he'd hear from her so soon. Hopefully things hadn't changed that quickly with her brother.

Knowing that if he offered to get George a drink and a snack, he'd happily join him for a timeout, Theo rushed as much as he was able to and the pair of them shot down the slide in parallel.

'Snack time!' Theo declared.

'Yes!' George did an air punch as if it was the most exciting news he'd received in his lifetime.

Theo enjoyed the fact that to a seven-year-old it probably would be. They headed over to the counter that was adorned with all kinds of jungle animals as decoration. He tried not to allow his architectural training to question why the giraffe appeared to be the same height as a flamingo. He had more important things to focus on, anyway. George's need for a snack first and foremost.

Once they had a juice carton and a packet of crisps, along with a banana for George and a coffee for Theo, they took a seat. It was time for Theo to give the message a proper read. He only had a short window while the food held his nephew's full attention.

It was a relief to see it wasn't the news that would break Kate's heart. Instead, it was almost the opposite... Matthew wanted to meet him! He was surprised to find the thought of that delighted him. Not only was Matthew okay enough to want a visit from a stranger, it also gave him a reason to see Kate again. The woman who'd only been in his life for a short while, but was filling nearly every thought. Knowing his respite from uncle duties was only going to be short-lived, he decided not to overthink it. If Kate's brother wanted to meet him, who was he to refuse?

He quickly replied to say he'd love to meet Matthew and, as she replied before George had started his banana, they made the arrangements in a series of quick-fire messages.

Theo was supposed to be seeing his grandparents tomorrow to do the usual weekend shop, but he knew they wouldn't mind if he delayed it until the afternoon. It was hard to believe a week had passed since he'd first met Kate on the train and even if the request was unexpected, it would be an honour to meet her brother knowing that it had very nearly reached the point where it wouldn't have been possible.

'Can we go back and play?' George asked as soon as he'd had one bite of fruit.

'You need to eat your banana first. You don't want me to get into trouble with your mum.'

See you tomorrow x

Theo responded with a final message to their rapid exchange. He'd offered his number to her in case she ever needed someone to talk to. He'd not expected that her brother would want to meet him, but if it was a reason to see Kate again, he wasn't going to complain. He just hoped that she'd be as glad to see him as he would be to see her.

Although it was never going to be like that, was it? How could it when her brother was dying? Instead, whatever this connection was, he was going to hold onto it. He hoped that whatever it represented wasn't lost when the tide turned.

Because the turn was coming. They both knew that.

CHAPTER ELEVEN

KATE

The thing that *should* have been terrifying Kate more than anything else right now was the prospect of her brother dying. Every day his oxygen saturation was lower, his body coping a little less, drawing them nearer to an inexorable inevitability.

So it felt odd to discover that wasn't what was scaring her the most. Instead, it was navigating the next hour where she was hauling a virtual stranger to come and be at Matthew's bedside at his request. She knew her brother's intentions were not all pure. She figured he was trying to have a hand in her love life... the one that didn't exist. But she found she didn't want to back out. She wanted to let this happen and go along with whatever might unfold.

Kate had chosen to wait at the same table where Theo had kept her company whilst she'd shovelled food down her throat only yesterday. They'd opted for this familiar spot as a meeting place. Every time someone came into the canteen space, her head popped up like a meerkat on watch. It was hard to put her finger on why she was so nervous. Perhaps it was because she did like Theo and didn't want her brother to make him run a mile. And there was every possibility Theo would run a mile as

Matthew had a habit of creating full-on embarrassment for his sister. It was easy to recall the times he'd cling-filmed the toilet for his own amusement. Or when he sent Valentine's cards to at least five boys in her school year, very boldly adding her name without telling her.

But that was back when they were teenagers. Surely such tomfoolery would have taken a hike at this point? Some of those memories were from their school days and, as that was a decade ago, it felt like an era they'd left behind.

'Hi! Are you okay?'

The butterflies in her tummy took flight as she realised she'd failed to spot Theo entering the canteen. He really was a handsome man and one that made her want to hug him every time she saw him.

'Hi! Take a seat... please,' she said as if he were here for an interview.

Kate didn't plan on taking Theo up without a debrief. Not that she really knew what to debrief him on when she was all kinds of nervous. Perhaps the fact that Matthew was struggling even more with his breathing than he had been the day before and that he needed his oxygen mask on at all times? Perhaps to mention that her brother's room now had a smell that she knew too well? She'd worked in the hospital long enough to know that the lingering odour of death had started to seep in. Or should she mention how scared she was? Of not only her brother dying, but of why Matthew wanted to speak to Theo? That mixed with the knowledge that she liked Theo more than she'd realised was almost too many emotions to handle.

'Are you okay? It was a nice surprise to hear from you, and I'm happy to meet your brother. That is, if you're okay with it?'

Kate discovered she was blinking back tears. She felt as if she should be passing Theo a get out of jail free card and here he was being entirely nice about her brother's request. 'I just don't really know what he's going to want to chat to you about and I wanted to apologise now.'

'You don't need to apologise.'

'But I might need to so better to do it now. And you don't have to do this if you don't want to.' Kate had to supply that as an option. She hadn't realised how uneasy she'd feel, but she hadn't realised he'd say yes.

'It's fine. I mean, I'm a nice guy. So it's understandable why your brother would want to meet me.' Theo winked.

It made Kate relax just a fraction, but it didn't settle any butterflies. He really *was* a nice guy. Normally when guys declared things like that, she knew that the exact opposite was true. But given the circumstances they'd met in and what he was doing now, it was one of those occasions when actions spoke louder than words. Or in this case, backed them up.

'As long as you're sure, we can head up.'

'Lead the way,' he said, with a warm smile.

On the way, Kate told him what to expect. How the room worked and what equipment Matthew currently relied on. None of the explanation made her feel any easier about this, but Theo's demeanour and Rupert the Bear trousers did help put her more at ease.

And she wasn't ever going to say it out loud, but she was beginning to wonder if this was a really bad time to start falling in love?

CHAPTER TWELVE

THEO

The last time Theo had been on a ward was when his father had suffered a heart attack. Even with the medical team readily available, he'd not survived.

Theo remembered the guilt of not being there when it happened. Not that he'd have been in a position to change the outcome, given he was only a teenager, but even to have been able to squeeze his father's hand one more time would have made him feel better about how suddenly it had all happened.

That memory was why he didn't mind being here now. This extra time Kate was getting with her brother was a blessing. When he'd driven her here from the train station just a week ago, they'd both believed they were venturing towards a point that was the end game. But it hadn't been and if Matthew wanted to meet him, Theo was never going to say no.

In a way, he thought it might make him feel better about not having had this opportunity with his dad. But despite that being on his mind, he wanted to put all thoughts of what had happened with his father to one side. He was here for Kate and for Matthew. And Theo was curious as to what he wanted to meet him for. He was hopeful that whatever it was, it would give him more reasons to see Kate, who'd become like a ray of sunshine he hadn't realised he was in need of.

Theo followed Kate down to a part of the hospital where he'd never been before. It was on the lowest level and seemed to be the furthest away from the main entrance.

'Don't get too worried... he's on the infectious disease ward, but it's because of the cystic fibrosis. All the rooms have been designed to have negative air pressure. It helps stop the spread of infection, but it also protects those who are most vulnerable. You'll have to scrub your hands and wear some protective gear when you go in. Is that okay?'

Kate bit her lip as she said it and the gesture hinted at how vulnerable she felt, let alone worrying about protecting her brother's weakened immune system.

'No worries. You'll have to talk me through what to do though.'

Kate tapped a PIN code into the door that led to the ward. 'He's in this first one.'

They entered a small antechamber-style room before reaching Matthew's room. It had a sink and all the equipment required. Kate explained what she was doing as she went, and Theo copied each step.

'The outer door always has to be shut before opening this next door. It's to ensure the room is able to do its job.'

Theo nodded, trying to take it all in. He'd not realised how different this ward would be to the ones that he'd known.

Ensuring the outer door was fully closed, Kate opened up the inner door. The pair of them looked like surgeons and the preparation hadn't been much different to the ones he imagined would happen pre-surgery. Theo was wearing a face mask, so he was disguised from Matthew, but Matthew wasn't disguised from him.

Kate's brother was propped up by pillows and had an identical shade of red hair to his sister, although much shorter. His eyes were a bright blue, again very similar to his sister. The combination might be considered rare if it weren't for having two carbon copies of the pairing in the same room.

'Hi!' Theo waved his gloved hand.

'Ah ha! Great to... meet you. Have a seat,' Matthew breathed.

Matthew gestured to the plastic chair that was by his bed.

Theo did as asked, feeling as if he was under the *Mastermind* spotlight without having chosen a specialist subject. He glanced around the room, taking in the medical equipment and realised there was no chair for Kate.

'Do you want the seat?' he asked.

'No, it's fine.'

'Kate, could you get me... some more... mints from the shop?'

'Really? That's the ploy you're going with?'

Matthew merely shrugged while Kate let out a sigh. Theo didn't know what to do with himself other than remain seated, while the reason he was here left the room. He missed her already. It would have felt easier if she was by his side.

'Thanks for... coming,' Matthew said, his breathing not always able to keep up with his words. 'And thank you... for getting her... back when... you know.'

'You don't need to thank me. I was just doing the right thing.'

'And as you've been... so generous already... I wondered if you... wouldn't mind... me asking you... to do one more... thing?'

Theo narrowed his eyes, trying to work out if this was some kind of trap. Matthew was so obviously poorly that he'd probably say yes to anything he asked, but he didn't want to make any kind of promises he wouldn't be able to keep. 'Can I answer that once you've told me what that something is?'

'I know you've... not long met. I wanted to ask... if you could be there... for her. For Kate. After... you know.'

Theo blinked, not knowing how to react. It was a big ask that was making his already racing heart reach a new peak.

'Won't she have other people for that?' he asked, almost as a deflection from how he was truly feeling. It was mad to realise that he'd already do anything for Kate.

'She'll have… her friends. Her family. But she won't… have a *boyfriend*.' Matthew was taking longer to get his breath back each time he spoke.

'But? I'm not…' Theo wasn't Kate's boyfriend. He should probably make that clear.

'Hear… me… out.'

Theo stopped, realising Matthew was getting too out of breath and needed the chance to recover before speaking again.

'I know she… doesn't have a… boyfriend. I know you… aren't her boyfriend. But it's… because she's never… had the chance.'

Matthew paused again to get his respiratory rate under grips and this time Theo knew he wasn't finished so didn't interrupt.

'She's always… been too busy… being my carer… to enjoy her life. To find… someone to be… more than a… friend. And I've seen… the way… you make her smile.'

'I don't know if that means…' Theo didn't want to make any promises he couldn't keep.

'It means… there's potential. And any potential… will be nullified… by what's happening… with me. I'm just asking that… you don't let it… escape. I just… want Kate to… have some joy. All I ask is…' Matthew took a deeper breath this time, allowing himself to recover with a long pause. 'Is that you explore what might be. And above all… make sure to never hurt her in the way my death will.'

'Okay,' Theo replied, uncertain if it really was. 'But I just need to say, this is all getting rather ahead of anything. I don't know if Kate even likes me.' Theo didn't want to admit that he really liked Kate. He figured she should be the first person to know that.

'I know... my sister. She'll deny... liking you. How can you like anyone... when your brother... is about to die? She doesn't have... the head space to... admit it's true. But I've seen... the glint in her eyes. I don't want that... to go out... once I'm not here.' Matthew's eyes were glistening now and if what he'd been saying hadn't tugged at Theo's own emotions that definitely did.

'Look, I know we've only just met, but am I okay to... I don't know, give you a hug or something? I've had to put on this garb, but I feel we should get past the interview stage if you're practically inviting me to be your brother-in-law.'

'I'm happy... to have a hug. And for you to... get rid of your mask... so I get to see... your handsome face.'

'I don't know about that.' Theo pulled the mask down rather than removing it completely. He then popped it back on ready to give Matthew a hug. He knew they were strangers to each other, but meeting him on what was effectively his deathbed and knowing all he was thinking about was his sister's well-being made it easy to like the guy. 'I can reassure you that I won't abandon Kate. I'm not saying we'll end up in a relationship either. I can't make any promises like that, but I think you know that.'

Theo had some kind of understanding of what it was Matthew was asking. He didn't want his sister to miss out because of what was soon going to happen. There were certain elements of that neither of them would be able to change. But Kate had Theo's number and he had hers. He would be able to check in on her and if she wanted to speak to someone, he'd be there at the ready.

'Like I said... if there are possibilities there... I don't want them... to drown.'

As Matthew finished his sentence, the outer door eventually

leading to his room opened. Kate had returned and they both glanced at her through the inner door window.

'Don't say I... said anything,' Matthew requested. 'She'll accuse me... of interfering and... even though I am... let's not make her mad.'

'Okay. What have we been talking about?'

'Our favourite PlayStation 5 games.'

'*Mario Kart*,' they both said in unison, laughing a little at their unintentional game of snap.

As they did, the door creaked open.

Kate glanced from her brother to Theo as if she'd entered the twilight zone. There was every possibility she had.

'What have you two been chatting about?'

'*Mario Kart!*' they both said in unison again, a tad too conspicuously.

Theo's stomach flipped at the thought of what they'd really been discussing. He'd made a promise to be there for Kate and seeing her reminded him why he'd found himself so willing to agree.

'Right?' Kate arched her eyebrow, a sign she suspected why her brother had summoned Theo.

'Yes, I've found... a fellow enthusiast... at last.'

'Matthew, every single friend you have loves *Mario Kart*. What were you really talking about?'

'Some things are... between friends. *Mario Kart*... friends. All nerds... stick together.'

Matthew put his fist up and Theo obliged with a fist bump.

'Nice to meet you, man,' Theo said. Not because he was being nice, but because it genuinely had been. It was strangely cathartic to hear someone's dying wishes and know that in some way, he'd be able to fulfil them. At least he hoped he would. He'd only offered loose promises because there was every chance Kate wouldn't want anything to do with Theo. He might end up being a reminder of Matthew's final few weeks/days/hours on the planet.

There wasn't going to be long for Matthew from what Kate had told him. The fact he'd been able to have a conversation with him was a blessing in itself.

'It's been great... to meet you. I'm ready for... a nap now, though. I hope... you don't mind,' Matthew said.

'Of course, I can show myself out.'

'Let me come with you,' Kate said, 'because of the door system.'

'Sure. See you somewhen,' Theo said to Matthew, a parting he used with his family when they didn't know when they'd see each other next. He didn't want to say goodbye knowing they might never see each other again. That would sound too final.

As soon as the inner door was closed, Kate started her questioning.

'What did he ask you?'

And Theo knew, no matter how many times Kate asked, he wasn't going to tell her every detail. He wasn't one for pacts, but given a dying man had asked him to fulfil a final wish, he was going to keep that to himself until he'd safely made sure it all worked out.

And, he realised, Matthew's request wasn't a burden. He *wanted* to be there for Kate. More than anything else.

CHAPTER THIRTEEN

KATE

Once they'd left Matthew, Kate wasn't ready to say goodbye to Theo straightaway. Not least because she didn't yet know what they'd discussed.

They headed to the canteen and Theo got them both hot chocolate on her recommendation and it wasn't long before she got to ask again.

'Spill the beans, then! I want you to tell me *everything*.'

'It was really nice to meet him, and he's not stitched you up or anything.'

'He must have. I know my brother.'

'He's just asked me to look out for you, so rest assured.'

'Is that it?'

'Pretty much.'

'Hmm.' Kate couldn't help but suspect there was more to it.

'What?'

'I'm not sure whether to believe you. Not because I don't trust you, but because I know my brother.'

'He just wants us to keep in touch.'

'The thing is I know he's trying to play Cupid.' The

problem was, normally she would mind, but perhaps this was the time to let it drop.

'And if he is, surely that's a good thing? After all, he could have filled the time with embarrassing childhood tales he's been desperate to share? All I'm saying is there are far worse things. He's only looking out for you.'

'I guess he is.' Kate flushed slightly.

'And if he is trying to play Cupid, it's worked! Here we are having a drink together.'

Kate glanced at her drink, then to his. 'This is *not* a date.'

'Oh. It's not? What constitutes a date then? Because there was I thinking we were on our third at the very least.'

'*What?*' Kate spluttered out her hot chocolate. This was a wind-up if he was classing this as a date.

Theo grinned at her reaction. 'I'm only joking. I realise this isn't a date. Not that I wouldn't want it to be,' he quickly added.

'I'm going to repeat for clarification. This isn't a date. My hopes and expectations would extend far beyond a hospital canteen.' Kate realised that, if it weren't for the circumstances, if Theo asked her out, she'd be saying yes.

'You're making out like I'm not the best company you've ever had.'

Kate shook her head like he was impossible. 'You know what I mean.'

'Okay, well at I least I know this isn't what you want out of a first date, even though, technically, I'm still calling this our third.'

'Stop it!' Kate batted Theo's arm and he grasped it to keep it there for a moment.

There was that connection again. Whatever it was that had led them into each other's path, it was here in the canteen.

They stared at each other for a moment and it might be the worst timing, but Kate realised she really did like Theo. She had wanted to ask him what her brother had asked again, but she realised it didn't matter. She didn't need to know word for word. If Theo said her brother only had her best interest at heart, she was going to take that and appreciate it.

'And on that note, I had best get back to my brother.' Kate didn't want this time with Theo to be over, but she also didn't want to be away from Matthew's bedside any longer than was necessary.

'Of course,' Theo said, with complete understanding. 'Do you want me to walk you back?'

'No, I'll walk you to the front entrance. That way I can remind myself what fresh air is like.'

Theo slipped his hand into Kate's as they walked and it felt so natural, she didn't even question it. It felt as if she'd found an anchor in the darkest days of her life. She was extremely grateful that Theo had come to see her brother. She wasn't sure she'd ever learn what their exchange had been about, but if it had made her brother happy, then she'd always be thankful to Theo for taking the time out to come and be here. Not for the first time even.

'Well, this is me,' Theo said as they reached the entrance.

'It is.'

'Let me know when you next want a canteen date.'

'It was *not* a date!'

'Of course... But let me know when you do want one.'

Kate held his gaze for a while and his eyes were the colour of the chocolate shop of her dreams. They were the perfect shade of dark brown as far as she was concerned. And she knew she was falling into them despite herself and the set of circumstances she was in. 'How about tomorrow?' she found herself saying.

'For a canteen date?'

Kate smiled and glanced at her feet briefly, breaking

momentarily from the intensity of his gaze. 'Not a date. Just for some dinner.'

'I'm still counting it.' Theo's grin beamed wider when she braved looking up.

It was strangely conflicting for Kate to find herself in a moment of happiness. It didn't feel like something that should be possible.

'And, yes. I'd love to meet you for dinner. I'll come in the evening, after I've finished entertaining my nephew.'

'Fab. I'll be here so just tell me when and I'll let you know if I have to cancel for any reason.'

They both knew there would only be one reason she would cancel: if she couldn't leave Matthew's bedside.

'Great.' Theo started to lean in to give Kate a kiss on the cheek.

It was hard to know what came over her. Perhaps an underlying fear of having put life on hold. Or knowing that she'd spent more hours in this hospital than she had ever spent clubbing or socialising. Or that she knew she'd forgotten how to live in the moment.

Whatever it was, Kate moved so that when the kiss landed, it was squarely on her lips.

She pressed forward slightly so Theo would know it was intentional. She wanted him to know she liked him and, despite everything, it was welcome. Him being here. Him agreeing to meet her brother. Him talking about dating in the canteen. They were all unexpected things that she didn't want to hinder. Life was doing enough of that as it was.

The kiss was fleeting, but it existed and as they parted, they were both flushed from the moment they had shared.

'Right. I'll see you tomorrow for our not-a-date,' Theo said, after they'd broken apart.

They both lingered as if the spell hadn't been fully cast, but it wasn't the time or place to do anything more. Not with visitors and patients alike passing through the main entrance with a footfall Kate wouldn't be able to guess at.

'I'll see you tomorrow,' Kate said, her lips still fizzing from their brief kiss.

'Call me if you need to.'

'I will do. Thanks.'

Kate watched as Theo headed off in the direction of the car park. She didn't want to say goodbye, but at least she knew this wasn't final. She knew he'd be back. Unlike the long goodbye she was experiencing with her brother.

Thinking about Matthew made her turn and rush back into the depths of the hospital. She'd been gone much longer than she'd intended. She normally only left for about twenty minutes at a time and now she'd been gone for more than an hour.

At least she knew the ward would contact her if anything changed. They'd been kind enough to issue her with a pager and they'd alert her via that if they weren't able to get hold of her on her mobile phone. It was because there were parts of the hospital where the mobile signal was poor. Despite knowing they would have been in touch, Kate checked both her pager and phone as she rushed back to her brother's bedside.

The pager hadn't gone off, but on her mobile was a message from her brother.

Have you kissed him yet?

It made Kate stop in the middle of the stairwell she'd not long entered. With the taste of Theo's lips still on hers, she didn't know what to think. She been so hypnotised by the dizzying effect Theo was having on her, she'd never thought the kiss could be manufactured. Had this been what her brother had requested Theo do? Had he gone to kiss her on the check because of a plea from her brother?

If Theo wasn't going to tell her what Matthew had asked of him, she was going to have to get it out of her brother instead.

It turned out the rest of her journey wasn't so rushed because she wanted to check Matthew was still alive, but down to the fact that there was a significant part of her that would quite like to strangle him.

CHAPTER FOURTEEN

KATE

'Did you *tell* him to kiss me?' Kate demanded after going through the process of entering the room with all the necessary infection control measures.

'What?' Matthew replied from his position on his side.

'You heard! Did you ask him here to make sure I don't end up as the girl who's never been kissed?'

Matthew moved a little, so he was facing her more directly. 'Did he?'

The temperature of Kate's cheeks rose and she'd never been happier to be wearing a mask. With any luck that would hide her blushes. It hadn't even been a proper kiss. Just a peck on the cheek that was given an upgrade.

'Oh my God... he did... didn't he? This is... *amazing!*'

'So you did ask him to then, didn't you?' Kate had come crashing down from whatever euphoria had existed far quicker than she would have liked to. Maybe Theo didn't like her in the way she thought he did?

'I never asked him... to kiss you. I'd never be... that blatant and... that would be... a gross thing... to ask. I just... knew you... liked him. And I knew... you'd never... act on it. So this... was my way of bringing... you together.' Matthew paused, always needing to catch his breath after more than one sentence. 'And it worked.'

'What did you ask him to do then?'

'I didn't ask him... to *do* anything... as such. I just... asked him to be... there for you. And to not... let any potential... go to waste. If there was any.'

Kate stared at him for what must have been a full minute. 'Was that really all you asked?'

'Yes!'

'I wish I'd recorded your conversation. What if you did ask him to kiss me and the only reason it happened was because he felt... *obliged*?'

'Can't you see... that's why this is... perfect? Because neither of you... had realised... or would allow... those thoughts to exist. And it's worked. It's worked perfectly. I've given my blessing. And you're... snogging each other... before he's left the hospital.'

'We did *not* snog!' Kate bellowed, a little too loudly given that their mum and dad had just arrived and were on the other side of the Perspex glass that looked into Matthew's room. But Matthew had really got the wrong end of the stick. It hadn't been long enough to include an ounce of passion. It was the briefest of kisses. That was all.

'Thou doth protest... too much,' Matthew quoted, then laughed a bit more when he saw their parents. 'Oh, this is... too perfect. I am... gonna die... a happy man.'

'Seriously, it was a quick peck goodbye. Don't you *dare* say anything to them!' Fortunately, because of the same procedure that everyone went through when they came into the room, their parents didn't arrive straightaway. Kate had to hope they hadn't overheard.

'When are you... seeing him next?'

Kate's blush took on a more beetroot shade that must be

going up to her ears. It was going to take more than a mask to disguise it.

'None of your business.' Kate stacked up her defences as if she were under attack. Then she remembered they weren't teenagers anymore and there was a chance her brother might not be about next week. 'Okay, tomorrow,' she confessed, reluctantly.

'Amazing! I knew... there was potential. But apparently... it was ripe and... ready for picking.'

'Don't tell Mum and Dad,' Kate said in an aggressive hiss as their parents finally started to open the inner door.

'Amazing!' Matthew declared as loud as possible.

'What is, son?' their dad asked.

There was a pause.

'Kate's horoscope. It's looking... very promising, apparently.'

Kate said nothing. She mulled it over in the corner while their parents greeted Matthew and made a start on his physio-therapy session.

She really hoped her brother hadn't asked Theo to kiss her. Somehow it wouldn't hold quite the same magic if he had.

But if Matthew was telling the truth, maybe his meddling had unlocked something that would change her life forever...

CHAPTER FIFTEEN

THEO

'Are you okay?' Theo's partner and best friend, Owen, asked.

Theo's body ached from another soft play session with George on Sunday, to the extent he was walking as if he were much older than his age. Kate had postponed their canteen date yesterday as Matthew had been having a bad day, but she had texted him today to say that her brother had improved and that she would be able to meet that evening if it was okay with him. Of course it was and he was already looking forward to seeing her again.

'Yeah, it'll be taking George to soft play twice in one week. The amount of times I've whacked my legs and come away bruised.'

Theo had known Owen since their university days when they'd both studied in London. Once they'd graduated, they'd gone their separate ways, but always kept in touch and visited each other for regular weekends. It was two years ago that they'd decided to set up a business together and they'd found these premises in Littleton-on-Thames. Theo knew he was lucky to get to work with his best friend.

'Ah, trying to keep up with George's energy levels would

definitely cause my muscles to ache. Probably every other joint as well,' Owen said with a chuckle. 'Maybe start taking the lift though if you are carrying anything hot or breakable?'

The office was only on the second floor of the purpose-built offices by the docks. As it was only two floors, Theo had always used the stairs to add a bit of exercise to his day. He didn't have a gym membership because his life was too busy to justify the cost versus the amount it would get used. So he had some equipment at his flat and did things like climbing the stairs to keep his fitness up. But Owen was right. Next time he went to soft play, he'd use the lift the following day.

Theo settled into his own desk space that only had two monitors. He'd always figured one per eye was adequate, not that he'd say that to his best mate who had four. He had his reasons for wanting more, but it was some time ago that Theo had realised they visualised things differently.

He was able to imagine things in his head with a far fuller picture, whereas Owen needed it all laid out in a very exact manner. Theo always did hand-drawn diagrams for clients, whereas Owen used software to create the design on his computer. Their different approaches worked in favour for their business. They would often both present designs, a bit like an episode of *Garden Rescue* or *Your Home Made Perfect*, and allow the client to decide who they would like to work with. Surprisingly, it didn't create more work for one than the other. The clients ended up divided between them around 50:50. It would seem that in the same way they'd found they liked to work differently, Theo imagined the clients choosing his designs were more fluid and Owen had the clients who were more rigid. That was a very broad view, but on the whole, Theo found his clients open to new ideas, whereas Owen's had very specific wants and needs.

Today, Theo had an artists' retreat to start designing and he needed to finish the Devon project, the one he'd been visiting when he met Kate.

Kate.

The woman he'd briefly kissed on Saturday. The trace of her lips and her vanilla scent were still with him.

He decided to open the Southfern project first so he could indulge in thinking about her some more. Especially as that was his favourite thing to do since meeting her.

Meeting Matthew had been a bit like opening Pandora's box in terms of his feelings. He'd liked Kate from the moment he'd set eyes on her. Not every woman would happily carry a deflated penis around and then when he'd found out why she was heading back home so early and the predicament she was in, he'd immediately wanted to help and had continued to like her. He knew he wanted to be part of her life.

If there had been any hint of lust, he'd buried it because he knew she wasn't available in that way. What was happening to her currently would always play top trump.

And it still did. Only he'd been told to 'explore the possibility'. He hadn't imagined for one minute that doing so would result in them holding hands and sharing a fleeting kiss. But it had happened... and it was as if he'd been struck by a magic spell.

Theo tapped his keyboard occasionally, followed by staring out the windows for long periods. There really wasn't anything further to do to the project he had opened, but he did need to send it off for planning permission and ensure all the details were correct. He was doing it one item at a time, rather than one page.

'What's going on?' Owen asked from his desk on the other side of the industrial bare brick office.

'What do you mean?' Theo wondered if he'd somehow missed an alarm sounding or something.

'You're grinning out of the window like a Cheshire cat. You

only do that when something's been going on that you haven't told me about yet.'

Theo did an exaggerated smile at his friend. '*This* is a Cheshire cat grin. I was just smiling. Happy, you know. It's not illegal to be happy in the workplace.'

'I know that and that's not what I mean. You're always happy after you've had your morning coffee. This was just... extra. So, are you going to tell me?'

Theo had no reason not to tell Owen. That was the bonus of being best friends as well as business partners. There wasn't much they wouldn't share with each other.

'The woman I dropped to the hospital...' He'd told him about that.

'Yeah, have you found out what happened to her brother?'

'I bumped into her when I took my nan for her appointment on Friday. Her brother hasn't passed away yet. Thankfully, the antibiotics worked.'

'So you're in touch with her?'

'Yeah. And her brother wanted to meet me, so I went on Saturday.'

'Really? Why did he want to meet you?'

'He wanted to ask me to make sure I explore any potential with Kate. He wanted me to make sure I didn't dismiss any possibilities just because of how unwell he is and knowing that he'll pass away soon.'

'Wow, man, that's *heavy*.' Owen shook his head. 'But hang on... why the smile?'

Theo's facial muscles set to full beam again and if he were able to, he'd kick himself. He really was going into Cheshire cat grin mode without really meaning to give so much away.

He really hadn't had a first date with Kate. She was right about the canteen not counting. But holding hands and sharing a brief kiss wasn't nothing.

'I don't know… I think something might have… *unlocked* between us.'

'*Unlocked?* What does that mean? Don't go all poetic on me now. Are you seeing each other?'

'She can't leave the hospital at the moment so it's not exactly been conventional in any way and I'm not sure when it will be, given how ill her brother is.'

'But? There's definitely a but. You have to tell me. I can't have you staring out the window like that all day if you haven't given me all the details.'

'We might have shared a very brief… *kiss.*'

'Aha, no wonder you're looking so smitten.'

'It was just… unexpected. And nice. But I don't want to get carried away. Not with everything that's going on for her.'

'So, when are you seeing her again?'

Theo stared out of the window once more. He had a feeling Owen was going to see right through him if he wasn't honest. 'This evening.'

'Really?'

'Yes, just for some food in the canteen. I think it's just giving her some light relief from everything that's going on.'

'And how do you feel about it?'

'About what?'

'About the expectation her brother has put on you?'

Theo shrugged. 'I haven't committed to getting married or anything that sensational. He's merely asked me to be there for her. Whether that be as a friend or a boyfriend.'

'I think it might have to be the latter. You can't really back-track from a *kiss.*'

'I know. Like I said, it was unexpected, and if it's making me grin as much as you say it is, it has to be a good thing.'

Owen glanced at each of his four monitors before replying. As if they'd give him the precise calculation of what to say and how to say it. 'Just go careful will you, mate. It's not exactly a normal set of circumstances that you've met in and that isn't about to change. It's going to be a really hard period for her and I don't want you to feel...' Owen looked at all four screens again as if they each had the phonics of the word he was looking for. 'Trapped.'

That got Theo's attention away from the windows. 'I know it might seem like I'm going to feel obliged after talking to her brother, but it's not like that. I genuinely like her and would have asked for her number when we first met if it hadn't been for the circumstances at the time.'

Owen nodded, seemingly satisfied with the answer for now. 'Okay. If you're happy, I'm glad, but I do want regular updates from now on. Let's add it to the morning meeting agenda.'

'I'm not telling Sharon about my love life.' Sharon was their part-time secretary who helped with their admin and worked there three days a week.

'Okay, perhaps not the official meeting. Just the post-meeting debrief.'

'Maybe you should concentrate on your love life some more and not worry about mine.' Theo was pretty sure Owen had been in love with Sharon for about two years. But because he was her boss, he hadn't worked out how to do anything about it. Neither of them was ever going to be willing to make the first move so it was like watching the slowest episode of *First Dates* ever. They were still at the bar and no one had ever managed to show them to their table.

'You know that doesn't exist. Can we agree that if I catch you staring like that out of the window again, I'm allowed to ask what's going on?'

'When have you ever asked permission? You know you'd ask anyway.'

After that, Theo concentrated on his work to avoid any further interrogation. He ensured every detail on the planning permission application was up and together to avoid any further queries from the planning department. He had every hope that it would go through without any delay. Once he'd done that, he finished working on the design for the artists' retreat. It was a commission he was hoping he'd end up taking the lead on.

Theo was beyond glad when the day was over. He headed home knowing that he was due to meet Kate at seven. And this time he was going to pay more attention to the clothes he wore and the aftershave he put on. Kate might declare they weren't dating one hundred times over, but for now, this was as close to a date as they were ever going to get.

With that vein of thought running through him, he decided to go one step further. They might not be able to go out on a date, but surely a date could take place in the hospital? Because despite the circumstances in which it was happening, Theo was very hopeful that they'd share more than one kiss in this lifetime.

CHAPTER SIXTEEN

KATE

Knowing that she was going to see Theo that evening was giving Kate's day some kind of texture. It was like knowing she had a bouquet of flowers on the way that was destined for her only. It was a change in the landscape after too many days of the same spaces.

Not that that was the focus of her day. That was her brother, because there was no denial that his blood saturations were continuing to decline and, even with the doctors increasing his oxygen, they didn't seem to be improving. And if they declined further, they weren't going to be using invasive techniques to try and improve them. Kate didn't like to think about it, but her nursing training told her they were getting ever closer to that moment. At some point, her brother's body was going to stop coping and it would be time to say goodbye. They weren't quite there yet, though.

She didn't want thoughts like that to be part of today's landscape either, but it wasn't possible to erase them knowing it wasn't just around the corner. They were *at* the corner.

Matthew hadn't been chatting as much today. His energy

was being better used on continuing to breathe, and making himself comfortable.

'I hope you're... having a shower. Before you... go for... your dinner. You don't want... to smell... like hospital.' It was the most Matthew had said all day.

'I've told you... it's not a *date*.' Kate recalled sniffing her armpit on a previous occasion in Theo's company. Classy girl that she was. She decided it was best to do it in the company of her brother this time. 'OK, you're right. I'll go and have one when Mum and Dad get here.'

'You could have one now. I'd be okay.'

'It's okay. I'll wait.' She didn't plan on chancing it, but she didn't want to say that out loud.

Matthew started coughing then and it was the type where Kate went to pat his back as the sound told her he was struggling to shift the phlegm by himself. It took a while for Matthew to recover, and Kate stayed rubbing his back, getting him the things he needed. This was why they weren't leaving her brother by himself. The nurses were too busy to know when every attack was occurring.

'Fair enough,' Matthew said when he was finally able to form a sentence.

'Shall we do an extra physio session while we wait?'

'Only if you... don't mind.'

'I wouldn't be here if I minded.' Kate rolled her eyes at her brother, but she wasn't going to push it further. His light was beginning to fade, and she didn't like it.

They went through the usual pattern of clearing his chest as much as possible. Normally it was carried out three times a day, but they'd do extra sessions when Matthew was having trouble.

When their mum and dad arrived, Matthew said, 'Go on! Make sure... you don't stink!' before their parents had finished preparing to get into the room.

'How *dare* you!' Kate said with an arched eyebrow and a smile. She hoped it wasn't the last time he would insult her.

Because of her brother being so poorly, she wasn't going to return home for a shower. She lived in a house share with some of the nurses she worked with, and they'd been fetching anything extra she'd needed. She'd asked for some fresh clothes from the flat, given that she'd been wearing the same things on repeat. It wasn't date-level effort, but she wanted to go to the canteen feeling slightly less feral than she'd become.

Having a shower in the hospital made it harder to detect if she'd removed the essence of hospital to the required level. But she used most of the products she had to make sure. She'd not really missed being in the flat and having her own space until now. She was lucky she was able to use the on-call room, but she'd not unpacked or made it homely, knowing it needed to be ready in case any of the staff needed to use it. Occasionally they had a patient needing regular care throughout the night, so one of the on-call staff would make use of it overnight. Fortunately, that hadn't happened so far, and she had a feeling, as this was work and her second home, the staff had arranged that other facilities were being used instead.

Once she was dressed and feeling semi-human, Kate headed down to the canteen. She hoped that her wet hair – her forward planning hadn't extended to requesting her hairdryer was brought in – wouldn't give away the fact that she'd made more effort than on the previous occasions they'd met. Not that there'd been many: leaving a hen do, bumping into him here, and at the request of her brother. That had been it, so she didn't know why it felt as if she'd known him longer. Maybe that's what happened with being in floods of tears on a first meeting. Perhaps that put things on fast forward.

If Kate thought that she'd put in some preparation, it was nothing compared to Theo. He messaged her saying to meet him inside the canteen as he'd already found a table.

As Kate headed up the stairwell, she wondered why because she knew the evenings weren't busy. Nobody wanted to be dining in a hospital canteen unless it was necessary.

When Kate turned the corner she saw that part of the canteen was darker than usual and Theo was at a table with fake candles flickering, a single red rose and two meals already on the table, which explained the message.

Theo was wearing a navy suit and, on spotting her, he pulled out the chair and held out his arm in greeting.

Kate gasped and her hands flew to her mouth. In all the years she'd been here either with her brother or as a nurse, she'd never seen anyone do anything as romantic as this. She wasn't sure how to react, but the first thing she did was check round to see if there was anyone she knew in the canteen. If there had been it was guaranteed that everyone she worked with would know about this in record time.

She didn't spot any familiar figures, but if anyone passed by, she expected they'd be down here like the paparazzi. She didn't know whether to be delighted or mortally embarrassed. For now, she was going to go with delighted.

'What's all this?' Kate asked, once she'd reached the table.

'Definitely *not* a date,' Theo replied, with the broadest grin she'd seen him produce.

'Looks suspiciously like one. Like someone's gone to some effort to convince someone they're on a date.'

'Take a seat, madam, if, *perchance*, it might be working.'

Kate would have protested potentially, but on spotting that he'd got them both the steak pie that was her favourite, she took the offered seat. 'The aesthetics seem to be correct,' she said as she took in the details of what he must have arranged as extras. Red napkins, heart-shaped chocolates and a bottle of red wine.

All of them were items Kate knew couldn't be purchased in the hospital so he must have planned this before arriving.

'How did you know pie was my favourite?' Kate asked as she arranged her napkin on her lap.

'From our favourite things questions. We covered favourite foods. Not that I expect you to remember my answers, but I remember you staying steak pie from this very place and how you were glad it isn't on the menu all the time, or you'd eat it every day.'

'I can't believe you *remembered*!' Kate had been practically incoherent that day she'd been so worried. She'd listened to Theo's answers, but she wasn't sure if she'd logged any of his responses in the same way he had.

'Please don't create a quiz about the rest. I might fail considerably. Just give me the full quota of brownie points for remembering this.'

'Oh, definitely. Is it rude just to tuck straight in?'

'Of course not. It isn't a date after all.'

Kate was glad she'd made at least some effort before coming down to the canteen this evening. She'd even put some light make-up on and some tinted lip oil. Not that she was going to admit to this being a date.

And would she want it to be if it was?

She already knew the answer to that as Theo offered her a selection of drinks.

'I'll have a small glass of red wine and some sparkling water. Thank you for going to all this effort.'

Theo had a carrier bag that was acting as a drinks cabinet. 'I figured there had to be some way of making it a bit special. Don't go thinking it'll be a nightly thing, though.'

'They don't do the pie daily. Only once a week so perhaps as a once-a-week special.' Kate smiled, but also knew that the likelihood of Matthew lasting out another week was beginning to narrow.

'I mean, it certainly could be arranged, if you are willing to confirm this *is* a date?'

'Let me check if we have everything on the list. Flowers. *Check*. Candles. *Check*.'

'Within what a hospital would allow, obviously. I wasn't going to risk lighting any naked flames.'

'Very sensible. Fake candles. *Check*. Added touches. *Check*. Oh, I know what's missing!'

'I thought I had everything covered?'

'If you're trying to convince me the canteen is now a romantic restaurant, you need music! Where's the tunes to create the right mood?'

'I can soon fix that.' Theo pulled his phone out from the inner pocket of his suit jacket. 'There was I thinking you wouldn't want any more attention drawn our way.'

'I mean, why stop at turning off lights and switching on fake candles. I'm surprised the supervisor hasn't told you off.'

'She gave me permission.'

That meant the entire hospital staff would know by the morning, not that Kate minded. Theo wasn't to know that the canteen supervisor was the purveyor of all the best hospital gossip. It was nice to have something different to worry about for a change.

'Thank you,' Kate said again, a tad overwhelmed. It turned out that perhaps it was possible to have a date in the middle of a hospital. Not that she was going to admit to that straightaway. Not until after they'd finished eating at the very least.

'I have to say, I can see why this pie is your favourite. I'm not always the biggest fan of them, but this pastry is just perfect. I wouldn't have a hospital canteen down as a place for fine dining, but you've clearly had the chance to research their best dishes.'

'I've asked the cook for the recipe, and she won't give it to me.'

'What's the best dessert? Because I wasn't sure on that front and the waiter here looks remarkably like me so don't get confused when he brings your choice over.'

Kate enjoyed another mouthful of food, not answering until she'd finished. 'Definitely the rhubarb crumble. Never fails to be divine, although ask for it with ice cream. The custard is always too thin for my liking.'

'Duly noted. I'll let the waiter know,' Theo said.

'What would you be doing right now if you weren't here?' Kate asked. She felt bad that she couldn't remember all his answers to the questions he'd posed during their first meeting.

'I'd be having dinner with my grandparents. I always go over there one evening a week and my nan always insists on feeding me.'

'That's sweet.'

'She really is, as is my grandad. Please don't tell her this, but I think the pie here is nicer than hers.'

'I'd never dare to make any comment like that.'

After that, they discussed various parts of their lives and Kate was able to digest more of what Theo was saying this time. The pager that was in her pocket was digging into her side slightly and it was actually providing some comfort. If it sounded, she was less than two minutes away from her brother's room. But it remained silent and by the time Theo was on his way back to the table with crumble and ice cream, it was the equivalent of a home run. They were going to make it.

By the time their bowls were empty, Kate couldn't recall when she'd last enjoyed an evening as much as this one.

'Would you like me to walk you back to the ward, or would you prefer to see me off the premises once again?' Theo asked, after putting a tray with all their dishes away in the cleaning area.

Part of Kate was desperate to get back to Matthew's bedside. She didn't like being away for this long, other than to sleep. Often she imagined the worst, having witnessed various examples of what was to come as part of her job. But she needed to wash those images away. She needed to appreciate the lengths that Theo had gone to in order to make another meeting in the canteen into something much more.

'I'll escort you out of the building,' Kate said, knowing that she wanted to be able to see the stars and, given all the romantic gestures, she was hopeful they might share a proper kiss this time.

And if the whole hospital was watching, she didn't care. In fact, if they were, she was hoping they'd need popcorn.

CHAPTER SEVENTEEN

THEO

The cold night air caught the hairs on the back of Theo's neck and made him shiver. The evening temperature had dropped more than usual for the summer. Or perhaps it was the company giving him goosebumps. He knew that he cared more about Kate than he had any previous potential girlfriends and that his feelings had evolved in a very short space of time.

'Have you ever seen a shooting star?' Kate asked as they looked up at the night sky.

They were in a very small planted up bench area between the hospital and the car park. Glamorous it was not, but if you ignored some of the surroundings, they could pretend they were in a park as they sat on the bench.

'I don't think I have. I thought I did once, but then my dad pointed out it was a moving plane and the star was actually a flashing light.'

'Do you miss him?' Kate was holding his hand and caressed his knuckles as she asked.

Theo sighed, the question having caught him off guard. 'I do. But I like to think his essence is all around me. He taught me how to be happy and he wouldn't want me to be sad because of his departure. There are days when I miss him, then something will come along to remind me he's there, checking on me.'

Kate stared into the sky, unblinking for a while. Theo wondered what she was thinking about, but no doubt it was her brother and what was to come.

'There!' Kate practically shouted.

'What?'

'There!' This time Kate pointed to the sky.

Theo looked up to the expanse they'd been admiring, trying to pick out exactly where Kate was pointing.

'Ah, a beautiful shooting star!' Theo smiled, knowing full well why Kate was pointing it out.

'I never knew I'd seen so many before.'

They both watched as the plane with its flashing light arced its way across the hospital and on to its destination.

'You see. The signs are everywhere if you know where to look for them.' Theo rubbed her palm.

After following the path of the plane until it was out of sight, Theo zoned in on Kate. She was starting to shiver slightly and he wondered if, like him, it was a combination of the cold and nerves. Things had definitely escalated to date level, but he wasn't sure whether he should try for a kiss. Not when he wasn't sure if that's what she wanted.

'I hope so,' Kate said, before leaning into him, closing the space between them.

As signs went, this was one Theo wasn't going to miss. She hadn't landed her lips on his, but she'd brought herself close enough to let him know it was his job to close the gap. At least that's what he hoped it meant.

Moving an arm around her shoulders, he closed in and kissed Kate in a way that would have made anyone watching think that he was thirsty. And he realised that he was. Kate was quenching a part of his soul that he hadn't recognised as being parched. They were two souls that had been giving up so much to their loved ones that they'd perhaps forgotten that they needed some love themselves.

Feeling her tongue slide against his was doing everything needed to help him forget that it was cold outside. It also made Theo stop what they were doing by pulling away slightly.

'I'm sorry. I'm about to get carried away far too quickly. And...' Theo didn't know how to say it's not the time or the place without them coming crashing back to reality all too quickly.

'It's okay,' Kate said, biting her lip in a way that would have made him buckle if he wasn't already sitting down. 'I'd invite you to my room, but as it's currently on the ward I work on, I'm pretty certain we'd disturb some of the patients and I'd lose my job.'

Theo laughed into the night sky. 'Well, we don't want that.'

'And it's not like we've been on our first date yet. We can't go hitting fast forward too quickly.'

'I'm telling you... this is date number *four*!'

Kate put a finger to his lips. 'Date number one. I'll grant you permission to call this date one.'

With that, he kissed her more gently this time. Like they had all the time in the world. Only they both knew that, really, they only had the next few minutes.

He reassured himself that despite the circumstances, there would be other dates to come.

CHAPTER EIGHTEEN

KATE

Bleep. Bleep. Bleep.

The emergency pager echoed out in the middle of the night and, even though it was two in the morning, it was so expected, Kate got up and out of the on-call bed as if she were partaking in a military drill.

She chucked on scrubs rather than getting properly dressed and ran like she never had before. The route was so familiar it was possible to do it on autopilot. She must have worn the tiles down the number of times she'd walked it over the past few weeks.

Don't be too late.

Don't be too late.

Those were the only words going through her head on repeat. She'd not even checked the pager to see if it was the ward trying to get her attention. She knew it had to be and if they were, it would only mean one thing.

This time her brother wasn't recovering.

As soon as she got there, before she was in the room, she saw his saturation levels on the monitor and knew they were the lowest they'd ever been. The lowest she'd ever seen.

She started the process of putting on gloves and gowns and mask, but before she'd finished cleaning her hands, her dad, Malcolm, opened the inner door. They'd opted to stay yesterday evening, perhaps sensing what was on the cards. 'Don't worry about that. Get yourself in here.'

Kate had always been so hyper cautious about protecting her brother, it didn't feel right to not be continuing with the usual vigilance.

But as she saw his bluish pallor she knew why. There might not even be time for aprons and who would want those layers between them in a moment like this?

Their mum was cradling Matthew, holding him like a broken doll.

Rather than focus on that, Kate tried her best to focus on her brother.

'I know this doesn't happen in most sibling relationships, but is there any chance we can call a truce?'

The corners of Matthew's mouth curled. 'Nah.'

Kate realised it was all he was able to manage. That the time for full sentences or even half ones had disappeared.

'Okay, if not that, can we agree that I'm right and you're wrong?'

'Other... way.' The bluish tinge blossomed into purple.

'Okay, brother. Have it your way and know that we've always loved you and always will. Go easy now and find your peace.'

Kate held Matthew's hand then, their dad holding the other while their mum cradled his head.

His last three words were like a counting down.

Three. 'I.'

Two. 'Love.'

One. 'You.'

And then there were no more breaths. No more words to be spoken. No more jokes to exchange.

Momentary silence.

Until the reality hit and Kate's mum and dad realised it must have finally happened.

Matthew was gone.

And Kate found she had to cut out the sounds of her parents' weeping to concentrate solely on holding Matthew's hand. Kate held onto it for the longest time, waiting until the heat was no longer there. She didn't know why, but she was waiting until she was certain his soul had departed. That it was no longer stuck in this room. That it had travelled to wherever her brother wanted to go and there would be nothing to stand in the way of that anymore.

Time passed.

People went by.

Nurses tried to convince her to leave.

But she wanted to be certain. She needed to have some kind of sign. Even though she knew there was nothing left of her brother here.

It was hard to know if it was minutes or hours that passed. But after her parents and the nurses had asked her to let go, she hadn't been able to. It took the familiar voice of Theo to snap her out of the trance she was in.

'He's gone, Kate,' Theo said so softly that it wouldn't have stopped a spider from weaving its web.

Kate gasped, knowing it was true and that it had been for some time. But she'd needed a sign and Theo was the one Matthew had provided. A last-minute gift to make sure she had someone to turn to. Her parents had each other and, of course, she had them, but in that moment she'd never been gladder of her brother's interference.

'We called Theo. We managed to get it from looking up his company,' her dad helpfully added as explanation.

As she released her grip on Matthew's rigid hand, she got up and fell into Theo's arms.

And she sobbed in a way she never would have in front of her brother. She sobbed because she'd always known it was coming, but somehow that knowledge hadn't ever made her ready.

Matthew was gone. And she knew it wasn't a graze that was ever going to heal over. This was going to leave a gap she'd never be able to fill. And it only felt fractionally better knowing her brother had somehow magically produced Theo. The man holding her now, even though every part of her wanted to crumble.

A final gift. The sign she'd needed.

CHAPTER NINETEEN

KATE

After Theo had dropped her back to her flat for the first time in about a fortnight, Kate didn't leave for the next two days. She knew all the funeral arrangements were already in hand, and her parents had said they didn't need any further help.

Without the regular routine of caring for her brother, Kate was lost. She had a vast amount of hours that were hers again, but she didn't know what to do with them. She'd lain for hours and stared at the ceiling. She'd scrolled through social media and indulged in meaningless nonsense. She'd cried so much she was beginning to worry her face would end up as red as her hair on a permanent basis.

In the end, she did what any woman with a broken heart would do. She ordered frequently from her brother's favourite Mexican restaurant, always ordering double churros.

She was now on takeaway number three and while she'd shed many tears, she wasn't drowning in misery the way she thought she would have been. She knew Matthew was at peace now. She knew he was no longer ravaged by pain. And because she'd known it was coming, somehow that made the aftermath fractionally easier. Not that she had anything to compare it to.

And eating churros in her pyjamas at three in the afternoon seemed to her to be the most reasonable response going. One that her brother would approve of, being that he'd been the biggest fan of the popular dessert.

She was also ignoring everyone and everything. It wasn't forever. It was just while she took a moment to get her head round the fact that Matthew was no longer here. She felt like she owed him that pause. She didn't want to go carrying on with life as usual yet. It was too soon.

Kate's ward sister had been great. She was deliberately on a zero-hours contract and had been since she'd started. It had always been so she could be flexible as she looked after her brother. It was nice, now that he had passed, that she wasn't being pressed over how many days she was going to be off and when she'd be back. She'd be back when she was ready, and she wanted to be the other side of his funeral before even considering that.

Reaching the end of her tub of chocolate dip with her last piece of churro, Kate decided to have a bath before her flatmates returned from their shifts. Making it as bubbly as possible, it made a nice change to indulge in some self-care. She hadn't done enough of that recently, only doing what was essential. So forty-five minutes in a bubble bath so high it was hard to see over was practically a spa day. Every time it started to go cold, she topped it up with hot water, thankful to be able to enjoy such an indulgence.

Once Kate was out of the bath, she felt more ready to face the world. Not that she was going overboard. Looking at her phone to see the various messages she'd received was going to be the extent of it for now.

Her parents had let all their relatives know, and they'd also put notices on social media. Because they were old-fashioned, a notice had gone out in the newspaper as well. It meant that Kate had messages from practically everyone she knew.

To make life easier, for now, she was only responding to the people who'd kept in touch while Matthew was still alive. That seemed a pretty basic way to prioritise who to contact. If they cared enough to check in with her while Matthew was still alive, then she was happy to respond to them now he had died. The others could wait.

Although as soon as she saw a message from Theo, she knew the rest of them could wait as well.

His arrival at her brother's bedside had been a shock and it turned out it had been down to her parents. When they hadn't been able to move Kate away and neither had some of her nursing colleagues, they'd opted to try a different tactic. An option her brother had inspired: they'd called Theo.

Fortunately, Theo had been happy to come by in the early hours of the morning and it had worked in unlocking her. Theo had been the one who'd dropped her back here, with promises to keep in touch.

For some reason, she hadn't been one hundred per cent convinced he would. There was something about seeing someone at the lowest point in their life that changed a relationship. It was very early days in whatever was happening between them. Despite what they'd shared, she'd half expected him to go for a stage exit right at the soonest opportunity.

How are you doing?

Are you okay?

I know it's a hard time so I wondered if there was any chance you wanted an escape? Just for the weekend. I totally understand if you don't want to.

There were multiple messages, which wasn't surprising given that Kate had effectively shut down for a few days. It was something she'd needed to do to help process the fact Matthew was gone. But he'd not called and badgered her and now was suggesting an *escape*.

She couldn't think of anything that she'd ever been in need of more. For some reason, cocooning herself away seemed to be her way of dealing with grief. So the chance to extend that only with Theo as company felt like exactly what she needed right now. The timing might be off, but she wasn't ready to face the world yet.

> *I'm as expected. Totally heartbroken and living off churros. But an escape sounds like it's exactly what I need right now. Can you tell me more details?*

Kate cleared all the other notifications at that point. Unless they were knocking at her door, she wasn't going to answer.

It was a relief to see that Theo was responding straightaway.

> *Can I pop over and tell you in person?*

Being asked after a bath and making herself human again made the answer a straightforward one:

> *Yes!*

The wait gave her long enough to blow dry her hair and make herself as presentable as possible.

When Theo arrived, Kate practically launched herself at him and the very welcome hug he provided. She didn't really want company at the moment other than Theo. He'd been there at the lowest points and was still prepared to show up when she was in need of support.

'Are you okay? I was beginning to worry.'

Kate breathed his woody scent in before answering. That

smell now represented reassurance itself. 'I just needed a minute to let it sink in. Although, I know I've taken more than a minute.'

'That's understandable.'

'It's been strange. I haven't wanted to see anyone, apart from having your company now. I shouldn't want to run away, but an escape sounds like the medicine I need at the moment. A chance to continue to grieve in private.'

Kate was buried in his chest as Theo answered.

'When we met, I was coming away from a holiday retreat that's looking to expand some of the facilities they're offering. The initial planning has been accepted and is likely to go through and they've offered me a weekend in one of their glamping pods. I figured with everything that's gone on, you might want to help me take up the offer? Obviously, you don't have to, but the invitation is there if you want to. They've said any weekend when they have availability, so it doesn't have to be this weekend.'

'Are you nervous about asking me?' Kate asked, recognising that he was beginning to ramble a little.

'A bit. I mean, I'm not sure if it's the natural order of things given what you've just gone through. I just thought perhaps it might be what we need. A chance for you to grieve away from it all.'

'I can't think of a singular thing that would help me more at the moment. I love my parents and my housemates, but everything here will remind me of what I've lost. I think being somewhere different will help. So when do we go?'

'As soon as you're packed for a weekend away? I'll drive us down there this time. It's one of those wooden pods so make sure you pack some warm things and some wellies so we can explore.'

'This is already sounding like exactly what I need.' Kate was happiest when she was in the middle of a field of sheep out on a long walk. It was something she hadn't managed to do in years.

'I hope so. I'm not sure what the signal is like out there so make sure you let the relevant people know what we're up to. I don't want people panicking about you.'

'I've probably worried enough people as it is. Shall I start getting ready now?'

'Yes. I hope it wasn't too presumptive, but I'm actually packed. I figured I might as well be ready in the hope you said yes.'

'Great. Make yourself a coffee if you want one while I get sorted.'

Kate left Theo to it as she went to her room and gathered everything she thought she would need. She went through the essentials in her head trying to make sure she didn't miss anything important: toothbrush, toothpaste, deodorant, her best clean knickers, phone charger, and wellies. She grabbed all of those along with the clothes she thought would be appropriate. She also picked up the book she'd been reading for good measure.

She messaged the people she needed to let know what she was up to and where she was going. She didn't want to make phone calls because she knew there would be conversations about Matthew and, as selfish as it might seem, that wasn't something she wanted to navigate right now. She wanted to shore up her own emotions before having to deal with other people's. Escape was her key focus to allow her to feel ready for when it was time for the funeral. She wanted this escape so she'd feel more resolute by then.

When they were in Theo's car in record time, she wound down the window slightly and allowed the wind to tousle her hair. Freedom to do as she pleased wasn't something she was used to and she planned to embrace it as much as possible.

'Have you spoken to my parents about this?'

'Why do you ask?' Theo briefly glanced in her direction.

'It's just my mum seemed very... *chilled* about the whole thing in her reply.'

'I might have mentioned it to check they'd be okay with it. I didn't want to presume without asking, what with everything that's gone on. They thought it would do you some good.'

Kate cheered at the thought he'd double-checked it was okay with them. Theo brought about cheer in her life generally and although it was not long after Matthew passing, she couldn't think of a better person to go away with to support her at this time. If they were dating, which they definitely were at this point, there were certain things she'd like to cement.

Like having a date outside of the hospital for starters. But Kate had a feeling as everything had been on hold, they were going in for starters, mains and desserts. And she was all for that. If she'd learnt anything this week, it had to be that life was too short. So even though she was grieving her brother, she knew that this was an opportunity he wouldn't want her to miss.

Especially given it was one that he'd created for her.

CHAPTER TWENTY

THEO

The past few days had been a whirlwind for Theo. He'd gone from meeting Matthew, to being at his bedside after he'd died. It was one of the saddest moments he'd ever witnessed with Kate in a daze, struggling to accept that her brother had finally gone.

In the days when she'd remained at home and he hadn't heard from her, he'd known she was grieving in her own way. He'd kept in touch with her mum and dad to ensure they weren't worried and fortunately one of Kate's housemates had been sending them reassuring updates, which he'd also had in turn. A round robin of care that didn't interfere with Kate's need to be alone for a while.

In between it all, he'd found himself vowing to keep the promise he'd made to Matthew in fulfilling any potential there might be with Kate. When his client in Southfern had offered him a free weekend stay, it seemed like the natural next step to ask Kate if she wanted to come. Her saying yes had made him happier than he thought possible, but he knew he needed to be mindful of what she was going through.

Theo wasn't sure what Matthew's expectations had been when he'd asked him to be there for his sister. At the time, he'd thought that it would just mean keeping in touch. Checking in with Kate in the future. Instead, he'd found himself in the midst of everything that had happened, not because Matthew had put that request on him, but because he wanted to be there for Kate.

When she said an immediate yes to the weekend away, he was delighted. Now he had a chance to get to know Kate more outside the confines of the hospital. And he hoped it would also provide whatever space she needed to help with the grieving process.

'I've not seen the accommodation yet. Hopefully it is up to glamping standards,' Theo said, once they were nearer to their destination.

'I've never been one to worry about sleeping under canvas. Do you know if they have showers?'

'Yes, they definitely do because I put them on the original design plan.'

'So if you designed it, you should know how much glamour I'm in for?'

'I know what the building *structures* look like, but it's so new they don't have pictures online yet. I'm not sure what they've picked for their furniture or how they've decorated it and, depending on what budget they had left for that, it can vary hugely.'

'Okay, and tell me... what's the bed arrangement?'

Theo had to glance in Kate's direction temporarily. He'd not wanted to assume, but at the same time he totally had. 'It's glamping for two, but I believe there's a sofa bed I can sleep on if you'd be more comfortable with that?'

Kate's hand landed on his thigh, and he instantly had to use every ounce of his concentration to make sure he navigated the last of the country lanes successfully. 'I wouldn't have come if I was going to be sleeping in a pod by myself.'

'Good. That's what I was hoping.' There was heat rising up Theo's neck. He'd never expected things to move this quickly, but he'd never felt like this about anyone before. He wanted to know more about Kate. He wanted to know about her quirks. What made her happy. And, most of all, he couldn't wait until he was lying in bed next to her. No expectations, just giving her the hug that he knew she was in need of.

But for now, he needed to put the brakes on, especially as they were nearly there.

Once they arrived, they were quickly checked in and, as Theo knew the place as he'd designed it, the owner left them to get themselves settled.

Rather than going straight to the pod, Theo gave Kate a tour of all the facilities. Everything had been done with the environment and the landscape in mind and the fact the pods were camouflaged with planting on the roofs was what had allowed the site to pass planning.

'My recent visit was because I was down here working on some plans for them to add a natural pool and some additional accommodation in the barn. We're still waiting to see if the permission will come through for that. Hopefully we'll find out in another month or two.'

'It's an amazing setting. It feels like I'm on a movie set!'

Once they'd found their way to the sleeping pod they discovered that there was a basket on the side with everything they'd need. Eggs, bread, butter, drink sachets and various condiments. There was also a bottle of champagne on the side with a card.

'Sourdough... my favourite,' Kate said, distracted by the array.

'I don't think this is something they do for every guest.' Theo opened the card that told him there was more in the fridge and thanking him for everything he'd done. 'And they've filled the fridge for us as well, according to this!'

Kate swung the fridge door open and inside Theo spotted milk, bacon, and sausages. 'We definitely don't need to call for a takeaway tonight. I'd say this is more on the glamorous side of glamping.'

Theo took a hold of Kate's arm, bringing her into a hug. 'Thank you for coming with me. It wouldn't be the same exploring this without you here.'

'You know we haven't explored this entire space yet. You need to show me the rest of it.'

Theo went on to give Kate the tour. He showed her the facilities in the kitchen and how it had been designed to be compact. He showed her the hidden toilet area and explained how the shower was outside and suitable for all seasons. 'And this is the bedroom area,' Theo concluded.

'It's amazing.'

'Well, like I said, the furniture and décor isn't something I'm involved with, but the owner has done a good job of sourcing as many eco-friendly materials as possible.' All of the furniture had been made from locally sourced wood allowing nature itself to be the main theme throughout.

Once the tour was over, Kate sat on the edge of the bed like a nervous doll and Theo's mind flashed back to their first proper kiss. Not the one where they'd pecked each other on the lips, but the one where whatever fire they had for each other had been unleashed for the first time.

Theo sat next to her feeling as nervous as she looked. He didn't want to rush anything with her.

Kate rested her head on his shoulder. 'Thanks for bringing me here. I don't feel ready to face the real world yet.'

'We don't have to here. Unless a field of sheep counts as the real world?'

'Sheep are my favourite animal.' Kate lifted her head and smiled a sad smile.

'Let's go for a walk in that case and we can make some dinner on our return.' It would provide a good distraction. He didn't want anything to happen too quickly.

As they got up, Kate hugged him as if life itself depended on it and he soon found he was doing the same. Whatever connection it was that had brought them together, Theo was thankful for it.

And he was certain, whatever happened next, it would gain Matthew's approval.

CHAPTER TWENTY-ONE

KATE

There had been a part of Kate that had wanted to grab Theo and test out the bed as soon as they got there. But the other part of her was feeling awkward and clunky and out of place. She kept having to remind herself that this was what Matthew had hoped for and he wouldn't ever view it as disrespectful for her to be enjoying herself so soon after his death. But that thought didn't take away some of the maudlin she was carrying with her.

Kate was glad of the suggested walk as it would help settle her mix of emotions. Once they both had their wellies on, with the light starting to diminish, they headed towards one of the nearby fields.

Kate slipped her hand into Theo's and concentrated on lowering her heart rate with every step they took.

'It looks like we're going to find that field of sheep you were after!' Theo said as they came over the brow of the hill.

'It's not a *baaaa-d* view,' Kate said as if she'd brought a terrible joke book along with her.

'Oh no. That really was bad.' Theo beamed in her direction. 'How are you feeling?'

They continued to walk with only the sound of birds chirping and the hum of grasshoppers filling the evening air.

'It's hard to explain.'

'I'm all ears. You don't have to answer now. We've got all weekend. And all the time beyond that too.'

It was a perfect place with a perfect person, but Kate knew she couldn't quite feel it because there was a part of her that was numb.

'I know I want escape, but I'm missing Matthew, like a weird ache in my heart. I have this strange gnawing sensation in my chest. Like somebody has hollowed my heart out.'

'I remember feeling like that when my dad passed. We just need to work out what your sign is. The thing that gives you a nod to that person keeping an eye out for you.'

Kate didn't know if she believed in things like that, even though they had discussed it before.

A sheep bleated at them as they reached the field's perimeter.

'*Baa* to you too,' Kate said to the sheep. 'And, no, a sheep talking to me isn't a signal from my brother.'

'Is that because it would be too *un-baa-lieveable*.' Theo pulled her closer, putting his arm across her shoulder.

Kate laughed at his equally terrible joke and relaxed into him, allowing some of the tension to release. She didn't know why she was feeling clunky around him, but she wanted that side of things to disappear.

As they stared at the field of sheep, they all seemed to turn and stare back.

'Do you think they understand each other? Because they're discussing something.'

'They probably want to know who we are.'

A red admiral butterfly fluttered into view and made its way over to them, landing momentarily on Theo's head before flying away again.

Kate didn't say it out loud, but she was going to take that as her sign and she knew from now on, if she saw a red admiral, she was going to regard it as a signal that her brother was watching over her. And, in this instance, she was going to see it as her brother giving Theo his blessing.

'What do you think they'll say if they see us kiss?' Kate twisted round to face Theo.

'I think they'll tell everyone that passes from here on out.'

'Is being the centre of such sheepy gossip something you can handle?'

Theo moved his arms around her back and the sensation flooded Kate's veins with endorphins.

'There's only one way to find out.'

Kate landed her lips on Theo's first. She'd been desperate to do so ever since they last shared a kiss, but the circumstances they were in meant it had had to wait. But being surrounded by sheep with butterflies passing by made it the moment she'd been waiting for.

The kiss started slowly until they moved to opened mouths and exploring tongues and their bodies pressing closer and closer to each other. Kate wished they were skin on skin, but with the way they were kissing, she knew they wouldn't reach nightfall without that happening.

They both stopped momentarily to catch their breath, but it wasn't long before they were locked in another kiss, and then another. If the grass wasn't so damp, Kate might have suggested they do far more than base one in front of the sheep.

An unexpected interruption put a stop to their display of affection. One of the sheep had a go at chewing Theo's coat as if it had been a goat in another life.

'Get off, you!' Theo had to tug his coat out of the way and jumped back as he did. At that moment Theo's knee gave way, meaning he landed unceremoniously on his bottom. 'Wow! Talk about bring a guy back down to earth.'

'Are you okay?' Kate offered her hand, half concerned, half wanting to laugh at the sheep's audacity.

'I think only my pride has been injured.' Theo accepted Kate's hand as he got himself up.

'We'd best get you back. I hope you brought a spare pair of trousers?'

'Give us a second. I think standing here for another minute will make me feel better.' Theo leaned in to kiss Kate again and she put up zero resistance. It might be turning a bit cold and the sheep might be protesting, but it was a moment neither of them wanted to end.

'Are you sure you're okay?' Kate asked again.

'I think so. And I hate to tell you, these are my only trousers so I'm going to have to parade around in boxer shorts from now on.' Theo took his first tentative steps, like an uncertain duckling just testing out his limbs for the first time.

'Really? Not that I'm complaining.'

Theo laughed. 'Don't worry. I do have one spare pair with me.'

'I don't think you'll be needing them as soon as we get back.'

'Now it's my turn to ask... you really don't mind me stripping to my boxers?'

'Absolutely not. I believe there's a bed we need to test.'

Kate didn't overthink anything from that point on. It was strange how sometimes it was possible to have an innate sense of whether someone was trustworthy or not. She'd known that from the start about Theo. Now she wanted to take things one step further.

And, somehow, it just felt right.

CHAPTER TWENTY-TWO

THEO

The shower was steaming hot, and was exactly what Theo required. He allowed it to cut through every portion of his body that required the heat. Falling onto his butt had jarred him more than he'd realised when it had first happened. By the time they'd returned to the pod, the cold had set in and he could feel himself stiffening up. Warming up his muscles was definitely needed, especially with how things were going.

When Theo went back into the main area wrapped only in a towel, he was in danger of buckling without the help of a sheep-goat when he discovered Kate in bed waiting for him.

Still wrapped in his towel, he found his way under the covers to join her.

'I wasn't sure whether to start dinner or...'

'*Or* seems like the much better option. You chose well.' Theo nestled into the bed, aware that he was still damp.

'I was hoping you'd say that.'

Theo kissed Kate like they had been doing outside before he fell over. It was deep and full of longing and the kind of kiss that he wished would never end.

He allowed his hands to explore and discovered that Kate

only had her underwear on. He waited until she'd tugged off his towel to then start taking them off so she was as naked as he was.

Kate was beautiful and he moved closer to enjoy touching every inch of her skin.

'Are you okay after your fall?' Kate brushed her hand over his hip and Theo's body was reacting exactly as he'd expect.

'I think the injuries are superficial. I think my pride has taken the biggest dent.'

'I am a qualified nurse. I'm sure I can fix all those problems.'

Theo had to clear his throat before answering. Lust was making it hard to form sentences. 'Only if you're happy to?'

He was going to make sure that was the case. He wanted to without a doubt, but he wanted to make sure it was the right thing for Kate as well.

'Would I be here if I wasn't?'

'It's never too late to change your mind.'

'Have you?'

'No.'

'Neither have I. Now let me check if everything is okay.' Kate travelled under the covers and started kissing every inch of his flesh all the way to his groin, then skipping to his thighs.

Theo groaned and struggled to contain more of them as Kate's lips danced across his skin. And soon it was his turn to return the same level of affection.

He was letting her take the lead and wherever she took him, he was going to follow. And they were both chasing the most pleasurable evening they'd had in a long time.

CHAPTER TWENTY-THREE

KATE

Kate knew there would be some people who might frown at what she was up to at the moment. Enjoying a full-on romantic weekend before her brother's body was in the ground might not be everybody's guide to grieving, but it was exactly what Kate had needed.

It was like this part of her had been waiting to be unleashed, and Theo had definitely held the key.

Now she was cooking sausage, egg and bacon with the radio playing in the background and she was humming along like she didn't have a care in the world. Perhaps because, for now, she didn't.

'Do you need a hand?' Theo asked, coming out of the toilet.

'Not right now. Maybe later.' Kate winked at Theo as she said it. She didn't know where this confident version of herself had come from, but she was going to embrace it. For some reason she felt assured in Theo's presence, more so than with any previous lover. It was as if two pieces of a jigsaw had come together and found they were a perfect match.

'Smells good.'

'I figured we'd need to eat after being too busy to get round to it last night.'

They'd ended up having a late night round of toast as their dinner. It was without doubt the best round of toast in bed that Kate had ever had. She figured she'd repay the favour by cooking for Theo this morning.

'I could definitely eat. I'll make the drinks.'

They settled into a steady rhythm as they both navigated the small kitchen space. Anyone getting in the way when Kate was cooking would normally irk her, but somehow Theo being in her space was okay. Soon the breakfast was plated up and Theo had made them both a filter coffee.

'The views are *gorgeous*,' Kate said as they sat down at the breakfast bar that could be folded down from the wall. She meant outside, but she was also looking directly at Theo knowing that was all the view she'd ever need.

'Anyone would think the architect made sure the pods were facing out towards the valley.'

'I think he must have done. I have his number so I can call and check if you like?'

'Nah. He's probably really pleased with himself for being such a good decision-maker. He'll be unbearably braggish.'

Kate brushed a kiss on his neck before starting to eat her breakfast. 'I couldn't think of anything that was further away from describing you.'

'What do you want to do today?'

'What are the options?'

'Go to the beach. Walk an alpaca. Go for a long walk and get lost?'

'They all sound like a brilliant way to spend a day.'

'Well, we definitely need to walk an alpaca. I promised the owner that we would as they're training them up to do it with members of the public.'

'Are we not members of the public then?'

'I think in this instance we class as guinea pigs.'

Kate dipped her toast into the yolk of her egg and did her best not to let it dribble down her as she ate a mouthful.

'I can cope with being a guinea pig, especially if it helps your friend out.'

'He'll be most pleased. I just hope the alpacas behave more than the local sheep.'

After eating their breakfast, they got ready by first lying in each other's arms for another half hour. It was a fragment of time that Kate wanted to hold onto forever. If she could place it in a bottle, she'd use it to return to time and time again.

Her brother had gone, she knew that. She'd been waiting for that to come along and puncture her heart for a very long time. But Matthew had made sure this was possible before he'd departed and she'd be forever thankful for that. And lying there, having her belly stroked like it was the most precious thing in the world, was something she'd never expected. Its surprising nature was a gift.

At some point, they managed to haul themselves out of bed and into some clothes to venture to the outbuilding and field where the alpacas were kept. If Kate had realised they were here, she would have ventured this way much sooner, although she'd been rather distracted by Theo's company.

'Thank you for agreeing to do this.' The owner, Harry, had a hold of two leads, an alpaca either side of him.

'It's our pleasure, I think! What do we need to do?'

'I'll get you to give them some feed to start with so they can get used to having you both here. We've trained them a lot with the walking, but they've not done it with any strangers yet.'

Harry spent a minute sorting the food and put some in Kate's cupped hand, followed by Theo's.

The alpacas didn't seem too worried at all about who fed them. Kate's was the smaller of the two with white fur and the way it chewed its food with its teeth on show was joyful. Theo's alpaca was taller with brown fur and kept looking towards Harry as if he were asking: 'Who's this fella?'

The feeding having been a success, Harry gave them both a lead and warned them not to let go, before heading up the walking party like a route guide.

Kate concentrated on the uneven country lanes they were going along while keeping an eye on the alpaca, whose name was Phyllis she'd discovered. She wanted Phyllis to know they were going to be friends and that if she just continued following, all would be well.

Theo's alpaca, Rocky, was definitely not as compliant. If Theo wanted him to go to one side of the lane, generally he'd try and move to the other side. If he saw any bushes at his height, he'd want to stop for a snack.

If it were a race, Kate and Phyllis had definitely taken the lead.

'Phyllis is ready to be taken out. You can see why Rocky needs more practice,' Harry said as they paused, giving Theo some time to catch up with his charge.

'He seems more boisterous. I'm glad I've got Phyllis.'

They both watched as Rocky tugged to lean across a ditch at the side of the road. Theo attempted to pull the other way, but it was pretty clear who was going to win.

'No, Rocky. Come on, mate. This way.' Theo attempted coaxing Rocky away, but it was no use.

'Careful!' Kate called, envisaging what was about to happen before it even had.

Sure enough, about three seconds later, Rocky went for one more determined yank and Theo's strong grip didn't have enough force to prevent it. As Rocky got his prize of a few leaves off the tree, Theo followed, falling into the ditch as he went.

'No, Rocky!' Harry called as he went to the rescue.

Theo had let go of the rein as he stumbled, and none of them wanted an alpaca on the loose.

Kate walked Phyllis, who happily obliged, over to Theo to try and help him out of the boggy ditch.

'Oh my! I stink so badly.'

'I don't think anyone has gone in that puddle for a hundred years!' Kate held her nose with one hand, using it to stop her laughter as much as to shield from the smell. 'Are you okay?'

'I didn't do it voluntarily and I don't think I am. I've never smelt so bad in all my life!' Theo laughed as he managed to get to his feet, covered in stagnant foul-smelling water. He tried to clean his hands down the untouched portion of his polo shirt.

'Hold onto my hand.' Kate allowed a peal of laughter out, seeing as Theo was laughing she was going to join in. 'We'll get you out, won't we, Phyllis?'

Phyllis didn't answer and nor did Theo. Instead he took her hand and managed to squelch himself and his wellies out of the unsavoury puddle.

'Ugh. Don't get too close, not now I'm a bog monster.'

At that, they laughed mercilessly for a while, both of them dry heaving whenever they got so much as a whiff.

'Have you hurt yourself anywhere?' Kate asked, once she was able to sensibly string a sentence together.

'I don't think so. I've just learned that lesson is true... never work with animals or children. They seem to be particularly hazardous if you've packed lightly.'

'Oh God, I'm so sorry,' Harry said as he returned along the lane having caught Rocky. 'You can see why I'm doing some trial runs. Phyllis will be fine doing walks, but Rocky's a law unto himself.'

'Don't worry, mate. I'm not going to add a review on Tripadvisor.' Theo managed a chuckle despite the state he was in.

'I'll take Phyllis and get them both back. You go and get yourself sorted.'

'Ah, I was getting attached to Phyllis,' Kate said.

'You can stay and finish if you want to. Don't let my antics stop you,' Theo said.

Kate caught a whiff of how pungent Theo now was. 'No, not at all. However much Phyllis and I have bonded, that doesn't take away from the fact that you'll need some help being hosed down.'

'I think it might take that kind of intervention,' Theo admitted. 'It's a good job the shower is outside.'

'There's a washing machine in the outhouse if you need to use it,' Harry said, before wishing them well and heading back with the two alpacas in tow, Rocky now behaving.

'Without doubt, I'll be needing to take up that offer,' Theo confirmed, before waving goodbye to Harry.

When they got back to their pod, Kate helped Theo off with his clothes and they were both thankful of the external shower as they chucked the trousers on the floor to wash off the worst at the same time.

If Theo wasn't smelling like a wasteland, Kate would have joined him. Even as she made them both hot drinks, she thought about the previous night and how much she was hoping for a repeat. If all they did for the rest of the break was stay in bed, it would be a very welcome development. She just had to hope that Theo managed to remove every single toxin he'd come into contact with in that boggy ditch.

They had one more night before they'd be returning home and Kate didn't want to return to reality. She knew that here, she was able to block out the knowledge she no longer had a brother relying on her. Being home would be a full reminder of how much her routine had changed. Of how many gaps there were to fill. It was going to take more than a minute to get used to.

Those thoughts were soon put on pause once more when Theo returned from his shower and invited Kate to join him.

Kate was more than happy to let the drinks go cold while she had the shower with Theo that she'd been dreaming about, the smell of stagnant water thankfully gone.

Instead, she allowed whatever was happening between them to fill the emotional void that she wasn't ready to face yet.

CHAPTER TWENTY-FOUR

THEO

Theo's alarm had gone off far too soon. Not least because it was no longer the weekend. What he'd give to be still curled up in a duvet with Kate once more...

Instead, he was faced with the prospect of another Monday. Theo and Mondays had a love-hate relationship. Sometimes he was filled with the sense of new possibilities. A new slate ready to be filled with all the things he wanted to achieve. On other occasions, they came around too quickly and only gave him the sense of being stuck in the rat race. Nobody was winning if everyone was after the same thing.

He already knew it wouldn't be his usual Monday start as by the time he'd driven back to his flat, he realised he'd developed a slow puncture. And he needed to get that fixed before heading into work. He sent Owen a message to let him know he'd be late and would work from home until it was fixed.

What? And delay giving me the gossip from the weekend? Unforgivable. :-)

'Of course that's what you're worried about,' Theo said

entirely to himself, seeing as there was no one else there. He'd dropped Kate back to hers, before realising the tyre was deflating and he was already missing her. He hoped his best mate didn't think he was bunking off with her, although if that had been an option he would have taken it.

He had invited Kate back to join him, uncertain as to whether she wanted company or some time alone after what had turned out to be a strenuous weekend with barely being able to take their hands off each other. Kate had opted to take up her parents' invitation to Sunday dinner. She'd invited Theo along, but under the circumstances he figured they needed some time alone together. An opportunity to start reforming as a family of three.

He realised when he dropped her off that it had been the right call. However much he'd enjoyed their weekend together he knew it would never erase what was to come. He'd already offered to attend the funeral and Kate had agreed that Matthew would approve of him being there. It was like a switch back to reality that neither of them had wanted to face, but it had been inevitably waiting for them once they reached home.

It was strange to have known someone for such a short amount of time, but to feel connected to them because of how things had worked out and what had happened since. Invisible strings that would keep them together.

'Right, let's see how long it takes to get this tyre fixed.'

It was a rubbish thing to have to sort at the beginning of the week, but Theo believed that bad things came in threes. A sheep-goat, an alpaca, and a deflated tyre meant he'd reached his quota.

Again, Theo wondered if speaking to himself meant he should get a pet to make the habit less questionable. If he did, he'd make sure it wasn't an alpaca. Or a sheep, for that matter.

Once the tyre company had confirmed they'd be with him in the next couple of hours, Theo texted Kate knowing that today they should finally get a date for the funeral. Messaging didn't feel like enough, though. He wanted to hold her as he had so often over the entire weekend.

When she confirmed the funeral had been arranged for Thursday and that she wanted some help on a shopping trip, he decided it was time to drop everything. She needed him and he was going to make sure he was there. He knew Owen wouldn't mind.

Yep, Mondays weren't his favourite. Especially ones that didn't involve waking up with Kate by his side. But he'd take the time off to be by her side if that's what she needed.

Because if bad things came in threes, perhaps good things only came by once in a lifetime. And he didn't plan to miss his good thing.

CHAPTER TWENTY-FIVE

KATE

It was an incredibly vain thing to be concerning herself with, but now the date was finalised, Kate really didn't know what to wear to Matthew's funeral. She wanted to be respectful, but she also knew her brother's wish had been for people to wear something colourful. Nothing in her wardrobe fitted the bill and, because he'd volunteered, she was taking Theo on a last-minute trip around the shops.

She was currently in a store's changing room with a red satin dress on that made her look as if she were a flamenco dancer.

'You look *amazing* in that!' Theo said when she came out to show him.

'You've said that about every dress so far.' Kate laughed. 'I need you to be objective.'

'You *do* look gorgeous in everything, though.'

'That isn't helping me make a decision. Anyway, this one isn't suitable for a funeral.'

'There you go. I must have guided your decision-making somehow.'

'I just don't know what to wear.'

Kate worked a hand through her hair and managed to avoid pulling it out.

Theo came over and placed his arms around her. 'You knew Matthew better than anyone in the world. You'll know what to wear once we find it.'

As there was no one about in the shop other than the assistant, Kate stayed in his hug for a while. It felt like a safe place to be while her head was in turmoil.

'The problem is I think Matthew would be happier if I turned up dressed as a duck or a pickle.'

'There's the issue then. We're looking in entirely the wrong stores. I know which shop we need to go to next.'

Kate got herself out of the red dress that would have been more appropriate for a cocktail party. Soon she was following Theo to a row of shops she hadn't even realised were in town as they were away from the main precinct.

'*This* is the place you need!'

Kate had been mostly joking when she'd mentioned fancy dress, but seeing as she was no closer to knowing what to wear, going in wasn't going to hurt.

The shop had rail after rail of costumes. Some in themed sections such as Christmas, Halloween and Historic. Others seemed to be a random selection.

'Is there anything in particular you're looking for?' the shop assistant asked.

'We're mostly looking for inspiration. Is it okay if we browse?' Theo replied.

'Yes, go ahead. And if you need to try anything on the changing rooms are just at the back there.'

'Perfect. Thank you,' Theo said.

Kate traced her finger along a row of options to see what was there. 'I think you should go and find your favourite, and so should I, then we go and try them on in the changing rooms before showing each other.'

'Okay. And no peeking to see what I've chosen.'

'Deal!' Kate said. They shook hands before heading off in different directions to go and find their outfits of choice.

Kate headed towards the food section. Even though she wouldn't wear it to the funeral – for fear her mother would *kill* her – she wanted to choose something that was in keeping with her brother's memory and as eating would have been classed as his number one hobby, she was going to dress as one of his favourite foods. Some of their happiest moments had involved food. She remembered getting into an ice cream fight once and their mum being none too impressed. And in the years he was well enough, heading to a local food festival where they would try as many cuisines as possible to the point of wanting to burst.

The costume selection reminded her of a food festival, although without the churros he'd always loved. There was a hot dog costume, chips, lobster, a burger or a bucket of chicken to choose from. Some of them were the type that required air blown into them, but it was an easy choice. Matthew loved a good hot dog so Kate took it from the rail and managed to negotiate getting it into the changing room without Theo noticing.

It was when she was halfway through the process of putting her feet through the bottom half that she began to lose it. Laughing so much that she lost her balance. What would Matthew think of this scene? And it made her realise that was the whole point. He hadn't wanted her to be sad and maudlin all dressed in black. Turning herself into a hot dog wasn't going to help her to decide what to wear to the funeral, but it was making her realise Matthew wouldn't want her shrouded in misery. He'd approve of her antics with Theo by her side, making her laugh in ways she'd never thought would be possible.

Taking some deep breaths to calm her laughter, she managed to get her arms through and her transition to a hot dog in a bun was complete.

'I hope you're nearly ready!' Kate hollered into the cubicle next to her. As there had been no one else in the shop, she had to assume the grunts coming from that space were Theo's.

'Just give me another minute and I'll be ready.'

Kate tried not to glance at herself in the mirror. She was concerned if she did, she might never be able to remove the image of the day she was a sausage from her mind.

'It's been at least a minute already, surely?'

'Just two more seconds. I just have a final attachment to add.'

'One elephant. Two elephant. That's two seconds.'

'Okay, maybe I need three. That's it, I think I've got it.'

'Can I come out now?'

'Yes, but with your eyes closed. I'm going to do the same and then we need to count to three.'

Kate did as he asked, although manoeuvring out of a doorway while allowing about a foot extra height was not the easiest of tasks.

'Are you ready?' Theo asked.

'As I'll ever be,' Kate replied.

'Okay. On the count of three. One. Two. Three.'

Kate was hugely tempted to open her eyes beforehand, but managed to resist. When she did, she laughed so loudly she almost lost her balance, the costume not helping. She'd not known what to expect, but it was nice to have something to smile about.

'Where did you find that?'

'It was tucked away in the rude section. It reminded me of when we first met.'

'Mum never did let me blow it up.'

Theo was quite the vision. If she thought her costume might be a tad phallic, his took the biscuit on that front.

'Look, they've even added *wool* for pubes!'

Kate bent over to look. Not easy as a hot dog, but once she was down she gave them a tickle.

'Don't go turning me on like that.'

'I don't even know what happened to the penis. The inflatable one, that is.'

'Maybe your friend reclaimed it?'

'More like the cleaners did.'

'If your mum didn't want the penis blown up, do you think she might not be too keen on my choice of attire?'

'I know our dating life would be over if you decided to turn up in this. Even if it would make Matthew laugh.'

'Is that finally admitting to the fact we're dating?'

'Didn't I admit that a while back? Why are you fishing?'

'Because I have something to ask you...'

Kate narrowed her eyes, trying to suss Theo out. 'Which is...?'

'Will you officially be my girlfriend and do me the honour of having our first photo together?'

'In these outfits? This is how we're going to preserve the start of our relationship?'

'Is that a yes?'

'You've asked two questions,' Kate pointed out.

'So it's a double yes.'

Kate felt butterflies in her tummy. They were there every time she was with Theo. At a time when she should be feeling sad, he'd made everything better. Nothing hurt as much as it should with him about. So she was going to say yes. A double yes. She had a feeling she'd say yes to everything he ever asked.

'It is a double yes. But only because you have such a good head on you right now. It would be a shame not to capture it.'

'Do you want me to take the picture?' the shop assistant asked.

Kate blushed. She'd pretty much forgotten anyone else was

there and wouldn't be making comments like that if she'd remembered.

'That would be very kind of you. Thank you,' Theo said, covering the blank that Kate was too mortified to fill.

They posed together as hot dog and penis and Kate had a feeling the resulting picture might haunt her for the rest of her days.

But she already knew that it would be one she'd treasure.

CHAPTER TWENTY-SIX

KATE

The day of the funeral was inevitably a much more sombre affair. After their tomfoolery with fancy dress, it had been much easier to find an outfit. It was as if she'd been overthinking it up until that point. In the end, she'd opted for a velvet navy-blue dress with a bright floral scarf. Navy was one of her brother's favourite colours and it felt as if she were showing her respects without wearing the traditional black like her brother had requested.

Following the hearse in one of the cars the undertaker had provided was surreal because she wasn't anywhere near as upset as she thought she would be. Her brother had been fading away in front of her for too long for her to be uncomfortable with death. She knew he'd reached a point where he welcomed the end.

She wasn't going to miss that side of things. She was going to miss the way he made her laugh. She would miss his competitive nature. And she would miss how involved he was with her life because of the nature of her becoming his carer.

'Are you okay?' her dad asked from by her side.

'I think so. I'm just waiting for the tears to hit, and I'm surprised they haven't arrived yet.'

Her dad placed his hand over hers. 'Tears don't always have to be public. We know how many we've spilled with the worries we've shared over the years.'

Kate placed a hand over her dad's, wanting to amplify the reassurance back his way. She'd not thought too much about how it must be for her mum and dad. She knew deep down, but the past couple of weeks had also been full of distraction.

'Sorry I haven't been about as much since he passed.' Kate usually saw her parents daily. It had been part and parcel of the routine of caring for Matthew. They'd shared a rota between them over all these years.

'It's a strange time for all of us. You're going on to new things or, rather, new *people* in your life, which is exactly what Matthew would want. It's exactly what *we* want for you.'

'Thank you,' Kate said, knowing both her parents were providing their blessing on the newest development in her life. It had been a strange moment to find she was falling in love. 'But today is about Matthew and celebrating his life and all the love we have for him.'

Kate nearly used 'had'. As if that love had gone away, but on saying the sentence, she realised that love hadn't gone away. It was still sitting in this car with them. It would still be there on the days that they all died. It was something that would continue on an endless loop.

'Yes, it is. He'll be happy knowing we're holding a party in his honour.'

That's what Kate tried to think of the rest of the day as... a party for her brother. He was at peace now and even though it was at odds with the occasion, it was also something to celebrate.

'How are you doing?' Theo asked when they arrived at the

church, and he was ready and waiting in the front pew as planned so that he'd be by her side.

'I'm surprisingly okay… The waterworks haven't arrived yet, but when they do, I hope you're ready?'

'Every pocket I own has tissues in it. I came as prepared as possible.'

Kate noticed that Theo had gone for a navy-blue suit that matched the dress they'd found for her. If she didn't know any better, they could be mistaken for a couple about to go to a wedding.

'My dad said today is about celebrating his life so I'm holding onto that as much as possible.'

After that, Kate held onto Theo. He offered his arm, and she took it gladly as they occupied the front pew along with her parents. She held onto Theo because it was what Matthew had wanted, but more than that… it had turned out to be what her heart desired.

It was later, when they had a smaller service at the crematorium that Kate's tears began to flow. It was because she recalled how she and her brother used to play together as kids. When they'd done things in a carefree way not knowing how things would change or what an effect that would have on the course of their lives. For a second, she wanted to snatch that back. To have that feeling return and be able to keep it. But as she watched her brother's coffin go through the shutters, she knew it was impossible. She also knew she wouldn't have wanted it any other way.

But now she would have to start learning to live without Matthew there and, feeling Theo's arm over her shoulders, she already knew she had the building blocks to start again.

But she knew she'd never forget her brother. She knew he'd always be in her heart.

CHAPTER TWENTY-SEVEN

THEO

Theo couldn't recall the last time he'd had a hangover this bad on a weekday. He was already regretting not having the foresight to book an extra day of annual leave after the event.

Attending Matthew's funeral had been incredibly moving, not least because of only knowing him in his final days and growing so close to Kate as a result. She had fared incredibly well. On more than one occasion she'd said she'd been doing her mourning for years and he understood that.

Once Matthew's dad had declared it a party to celebrate Matthew's life, everyone had taken that as a green flag to do exactly that. Theo had never been to a funeral that had involved as much dancing as a wedding, but that was the direction the occasion had taken and he'd been happily swept along.

Now his body was telling him he may have overdone it, especially without the needed recovery time.

The other thing he hadn't accounted for was not wanting to leave Kate. She'd stayed over at his flat – another reason for regretting not booking the rest of the week off. Having drunk more than enough to celebrate a life well lived, they'd opted to get a taxi back to his flat given that it was the nearest. He'd do anything to remain in bed with her, but there were customers booked in to see their project proposal presentations. He would be putting forward his bid for the artists' retreat and another project.

Kate had stirred enough for him to say goodbye, but he would have done anything to stay with her. What kind of lunatic only booked part of the week off? A workaholic was probably the answer. At least she'd known that was the case, though, before they'd crashed into heavy sleep, but that didn't make the leaving process any easier.

Theo pressed the lift button to take him up to the offices. It was not a day for using the stairs.

When he reached the office there was a takeaway coffee waiting for him.

'I thought you might need that this morning,' Owen said. 'How was it?'

Theo waited until he was in his office chair before answering. 'It was how I'd hope my funeral would be, so I guess that's as good as it can get.'

'How did Kate hold up?'

'She did really well. The whole family did, but even I shed a tear, and I didn't meet him long ago. But they treated it as a celebration of life, and I wish all such occasions were that joyful.'

'It's a much better ending than the one where you didn't know what had happened when you dropped Kate off the first time.'

'Very true.' Theo picked up his coffee and had a long slurp on realising it was just the right temperature. 'Thanks for this. It's one hundred per cent needed today. I rather wish in hindsight that I'd booked the day off.'

'You have my full permission to slink off as soon as we've finished this afternoon's presentations. And seriously, if you need to, we can reschedule.'

Theo took another slurp of coffee and thought on it for a moment. The issue with being co-owners of a business with his best mate was that he knew him too well. It also required hard work to make sure it ticked over.

'I think pressing on is the best thing to do today. However much I love spending time with Kate, I have a feeling she'll want to be alone with her parents today.'

For the rest of the morning, they both clicked and tapped away in preparation for the afternoon. They always tended to do presentations to clients on a Friday afternoon. Generally speaking, it gave them the whole week to prepare and everyone was in a better mood on a Friday afternoon and they had found it was the day that worked best for securing clients. As a business model it seemed to work and so they stuck to it. Today would hopefully secure another two projects.

As Theo got into the nitty gritty of the Pattersons' brief, he was annoyed he'd not given himself more time to create his presentation. He'd thought it was a straightforward extension and more suited to Owen's skillset so he'd concentrated on the artists' retreat. But on reading the finer details, the extension was to make modifications to the house on learning Mr Patterson's diagnosis of Parkinson's disease. They wanted the ability to live downstairs when the time came.

It was the kind of project Theo loved. It gave him the opportunity to demonstrate the versatility of the space they had, while at the same time giving him more job satisfaction than the average extension would. He did as much as he was able to with the half day that he'd given himself, but it was no surprise that, when it came to presentations, Owen's was head and shoulders ahead of his.

The reverse was true of the artists' retreat where Theo was the one who had put in more time and effort.

The back-to-back presentations were both excellent. Or at least the clients had said they were, and he chose to believe them. Even though they always gave the clients the option of having some time to mull them over and a presentation pack to go away with, both sets of clients had made up their mind there and then. It was no surprise that he'd landed the artists' retreat and Owen was going to be working on the extension, with particular focus on adaptable accommodation.

It was a relief to be at the end of the working day. His slight hangover had provided a mild headache throughout and his desire to return home had never been stronger. Not least because he was hoping Kate might still be there. That he'd return home to find her nestled between the sheets ready for him to join her. Although he realised such things should be filed under fantasy.

It was only once he was back at the flat, he knew that was true. Kate's coat and bag were no longer by the door. Instead, there was a note on the breakfast bar letting him know she'd gone to see her parents and she was looking forward to seeing him again soon. He called her for a brief chat and they both agreed they needed to take the rest of the day to get over their hangovers.

Feeling shattered, there was only one thing for it. Theo stripped down to his boxer shorts and took himself back to bed. He needed the rest, but more than that... he wanted to smell the essence of Kate on his bed sheets.

He went to sleep dreaming of the next time she'd be beside him.

CHAPTER TWENTY-EIGHT

KATE

Kate had always feared the aftermath of Matthew's death. She'd always known that she'd have an incredibly large hole to fill and she'd imagined herself listless not knowing what to do.

Perhaps Matthew had known that when he'd had a go at being Cupid and scored a goal with his first arrow.

Instead of being maudlin, Kate was spending time with Theo. They'd been hanging out with each other whenever they had the chance and had participated in some more regular dates: the cinema, bowling, a meal at a pub. Often finishing by returning to Theo's flat over Kate's house share.

This evening, Kate was about to meet Theo's sister, Anita, for the first time for a meal out. Anita hadn't wanted Kate to meet her son, George, straightaway, and Kate knew why. It was in case things didn't last. It would be horrid to meet the kid one minute and for her not to be about the next. She was being sussed out on this meeting, she knew that. And she didn't mind the cautiousness. Everything had happened at a quicker than average pace. They'd gone from being complete strangers to a couple who went on weekends away together in less than a month. They certainly weren't going to be the first or last couple to go into a relationship at that pace and the circumstances of how they'd met and come together seemed to have set them into fast-forward mode.

'Lovely to meet you,' Kate said as soon as they arrived at the Indian restaurant Theo had booked.

'It's great to meet you as well.' Anita got up and gave Kate a warm hug with a kiss on either cheek thrown in for good measure. The reception was so friendly it made the tension in her shoulders release a little.

'So tell me all about yourself! I want to know everything about the woman who's been holding my brother's attention.'

Kate glanced over to Theo, trying to gauge if he'd told his sister anything about her.

'What would you like to know?'

'Where you've *been* for starters? I've been patiently waiting for him to meet someone for *years*.'

Kate smiled and knew she was beginning to blush so she answered quickly in the hope it would distract from any signs of nervousness. 'I'm a nurse so I work bank shifts for the respiratory ward there. I'm sure Theo has told you that my brother had cystic fibrosis and passed away recently.' An unexpected lump in her throat formed. It was the first time she'd had to tell someone who might not have known and it was too soon to say those words without it hurting.

'He did. I'm really sorry to hear that.'

'So tell me about you? The things Theo has told me have mainly revolved around George.' Kate wanted to divert away from the subject of Matthew. In her current state, it was going to be the best thing to do. She didn't want to burst into tears on her first interaction with Theo's sister.

'Ha! That's so true. The same with my mum. Since George came along, he's the main focus of attention. So I'm a single mum to George as you probably already know. Alongside that, I work as a receptionist at the local primary school that George attends. It's really handy as my working hours are the ones when he's there and I get the same holidays off as he does. The only days I have to get cover are on school inset days and if he's ever poorly.'

'That sounds ideal.'

'It really is.'

The conversation about what they both did was interrupted by the waiter coming along and taking their orders.

'So my brother dearest is very good and normally covers some of the inset days, as well as taking George out at least one day of the weekend for a few hours. It's the only time I get any me time. It's a blessing that I don't know what I'd do without.'

Kate noted what she was saying because it occurred to her that the dawn of Theo's new relationship must have had a knock-on effect over the past few weeks.

'I'd love to meet George at some point, but only when you feel it's appropriate.'

'You do realise you're signing yourself up for soft play if you make promises like that.' Theo squeezed Kate's knee under the table.

'It won't be the weirdest date we've been on, but I'm not sure your sister needs to know that.'

'I'm not going to ask any probing questions on that matter now you've said that.'

'That's not like you, Anita. The good news is I have the photo to show you.'

'Oh no! Not that one.' Kate knew exactly which picture he was about to produce.

'Oh God!' Anita exclaimed when she saw the picture. 'What an earth were you up to?'

What followed was a rather long and complicated explanation which had them all laughing while their food started to arrive and they all tucked in.

The rest of the evening passed with Anita hauling out all of the embarrassing stories she had on her brother. It turned out to be quite a few, all of them equally funny and ridiculous and it seemed that his sister had been waiting for this opportunity to share them.

Kate found herself sharing stories of some of the antics she and Matthew used to get up to and she discovered it was rather cathartic sharing bits about their life as siblings. It strengthened that sense of connection that she shared with Theo.

By the end of the evening, she knew that she really liked Anita. That if she'd met her in other circumstances that they would be friends. But rather than that, instead, it was like gaining a sister.

'I'm going to pop to use the ladies before we go.' Kate excused herself from the table and realised she was slightly drunk as she made her way to the loo.

Once she returned, Kate heard Theo and Anita deep in conversation. The screens between each booth were disguising her return and she slowed down, wanting to hear a little of what they were discussing.

'She's a good egg. Make sure you look after her,' Anita was murmuring.

'I know. She's a keeper, that's for sure,' Theo replied with a nod.

'All finished,' Kate offered on her return. She had to hope she wasn't blushing again to give away the fact she'd overheard a small snippet. What Theo had said made happiness blossom inside her in a way she wouldn't have thought possible so soon after losing Matthew.

'I've settled the bill so let's head home.'

They all traipsed to Theo's car as he'd volunteered to be the designated driver. They dropped Anita off first and Kate got out to give her a hug to say goodbye properly.

'Where to, me lady?' Theo joked as if he was a character from *Thunderbirds*.

They weren't routinely in the habit of spending every night together, but it was becoming more frequent.

'Home, Parker. And I think tonight that home is yours. If that's okay?'

'That's what I was really hoping you'd say. I think it might be time I find you your own drawer.'

'I'd like that.'

Kate knew that at a time in her life when she should be sad, Theo was making her happy. Very happy indeed. She knew he was a keeper too.

CHAPTER TWENTY-NINE

THEO

Theo was floating on a cloud. If anyone wanted to burst his bubble, it would be impossible because of how high he was soaring.

He'd woken up before his alarm. It was as if his body was trained to know the exact time it needed to get up so that he'd get to work on time. Because he was wide awake and had an extra five minutes, he switched off his alarm and watched Kate sleeping.

Her black eyelashes were fluttering as if she was having a dream and he hoped it was a good one. He carried on watching her for a while, appreciating how beautiful she was. He'd always been too busy to want a long-term girlfriend. Perhaps he'd been self-absorbed, but none of them had ever held his interest. His family were his priority and often that seemed to put women off.

Kate was proving to be an entirely different experience and it was one that he was loving. The fact his sister approved was like the icing on the cake. He wasn't going to introduce Kate to George straightaway, but as soon as Anita gave him the green light he would.

Sadly he couldn't remain in bed. He wanted to. He wanted to make love to her again the way they had last night and enjoy an entire lazy day together. But, unfortunately, another week of work called.

However much he wanted to bend the rules as his own boss, he also knew how pissed off he would be at Owen if he started pulling stunts like that. The reason OT Architects did well was because of the amount of hours they put into it. They didn't go mad working beyond normal office hours, but keeping to those normal office hours was the least Theo could do, especially after taking some last-minute days off recently.

Despite knowing that, it was still a hardship to finally haul himself out of bed and into the shower. The cloud he'd been floating on seemed to disintegrate somewhat. It was that Monday feeling again. He was going to choose to believe it was a blank slate kind of Monday with plenty of opportunities about to come his way.

He managed to get dressed without disturbing Kate, but he did plant a kiss on her forehead before leaving and left a short note on the breakfast bar saying to stay as long as she wanted and to help herself to anything from the cupboards.

Part of him hoped she would still be there on his return. He knew that wasn't a reasonable hope though given that they didn't live together and she had her things at her house share. He also knew she had some shifts this week. The first she'd taken on since her brother had passed away.

He realised that he'd never seen her in her nurse's uniform and the thought immediately brightened his morning, knowing he had something to look forward to. In fact, he realised he had a lot to look forward to with Kate. He didn't want to get too ahead of himself, but everything seemed to be heading in that direction.

Theo stopped and picked up coffees on his way in. It was something he and Owen took turns with on a Monday morning.

A good way to kick-start the week. Or rather a much needed one.

The morning wasn't overly busy. They were wrapping up the contracts they'd presented for on Friday and once they had been signed and agreed, Theo would start the work to get the planning permission application in for the artists' retreat.

Their receptionist, Sharon, was in the office, and Theo amused himself by keeping a score chart of how many times Owen flirted with her and she responded in kind. The chemistry between them and Owen's complete denial of it existing was painful to witness. At some point he expected them to admit it and there'd be sudden passionate kissing across the desk and he'd have to leave the room swiftly.

Shaking that image from his mind, he attempted to concentrate on the work in front of him, but a buzzer sounded indicating there was someone downstairs for their office.

Sharon went to the speakerphone to reply.

'OT Architects, how can I help?'

'Parcel to sign,' an impatient voice declared.

'I'll be back soon. The lift is playing up a bit today by the way,' Sharon said, about to head downstairs.

'It's okay. I'll do it,' Theo volunteered. It was a good excuse to move from his desk and he knew the duo he was leaving behind weren't going to argue if it gave them five more minutes together. Some days Theo was tempted to suggest a desk change if it didn't negate the reason they had a receptionist.

The sun was shining in the stairwell and it made Theo want to head out and have lunch in the sunshine. Maybe he could message Kate and see if she was free to join him.

It was when he had that thought that it happened.

His knee fully gave way.

He was holding the rail, but his grip wasn't tight enough to stop it.

Before he was able to react, he was falling.

But as the ground wasn't there to stop him, he continued to tumble.

Stair after stair that whacked every inch of his body.

His elbow. His side. His other knee.

His vision went hazy. Dizziness from each spin took over.

And then the world went black.

CHAPTER THIRTY

THEO

When his eyes opened again, it was like his body had played wind the bobbin up. Every muscle in his body hurt and his palm felt wet and without checking, he knew he must be bleeding from somewhere.

He was curled in the foetal position with his eyes closed, but he heard the commotion from upstairs that soon followed. Doors opening. Exclamations shouted. Feet thundering down the stairs.

Owen reached him first. 'Oh my goodness, Theo! Quick, Sharon, get the first aid kit.'

'I'm calling an ambulance as well.'

Theo heard more doors opening and closing, but he was busy concentrating on his breathing. He was gradually able to draw more air into his lungs, although each breath pinched in a way he'd never experienced. He wouldn't be surprised to find he'd broken a rib on his way down.

'Can you hear me, mate?' Owen asked.

Theo managed to nod his head, even though moving hurt.

'Shouldn't we be keeping him still?' Sharon asked on her return. 'That's what the operator has told us to do.'

Theo did as suggested and remained still, continuing to get his breath back and allowing Owen to put gauze on the wound on his arm to stop it bleeding. He couldn't see how bad it was, but it couldn't be too bad if Owen's first aid skills were adequate. They'd attended a course, but none of them had ever had to exercise any of the skills they'd learned.

'Hopefully that'll hold up. Are you bleeding from anywhere else?' Owen asked, before proceeding to do a visual inspection of all quarters of Theo's body.

'I don't think so,' he managed to whisper.

'The ambulance will be here soon,' Sharon added.

Before Theo was fully aware again, he was strapped up and stretchered into the back of an ambulance.

'We're closing the office for the day. Sharon can lock up. I'm coming with you in the ambulance.' It turned out Owen could be quite authoritative when he needed to be.

The journey there and the arrival was a daze for Theo. They were taken directly to a bed space where a nurse practitioner started to assess his injuries.

In between checks, Owen tended to him while they waited and he drifted off intermittently, suddenly tired from the morning he'd had. There were various parts of his body where bruises were beginning to swell and still he didn't know if he'd done anything that would slow him down for a while.

'Good afternoon, I'm Doctor Redhill. Is it okay if I come and check you over?' The man in the lab coat introduced himself after pulling back the curtain.

Theo woke from his stupor. He'd not been in a deep sleep, but had found himself unimaginably tired from the earlier event. 'Yes, yes.'

'Do you want to go through what happened with me?'

What followed was a long explanation about how his knee had been troubling him occasionally, but this time it had really done him a disservice.

The doctor cleared his spine and went on to examine his knee, pulling it this way and that and he explained what he was checking for as he went.

'I'm going to get one of my senior colleagues to come and double-check some things,' he said once he had finished.

The curtain fluttered as the doctor made his way out and Theo stared at it wondering why a more senior doctor was required.

'You're in the right place, mate.' Owen squeezed his shoulder, perhaps sensing what was going through his mind.

'I hope so.'

Soon the A&E consultant came and did a repeat performance of the same tests.

'You're correct, Doctor Redhill. Check over everything else, then we'll put in a call to the on-call neuro team so they can see Theo before he goes home.' The consultant headed out of the cubicle with the same energy he had turned up with, not giving Theo any indication as to what any of that meant. Theo imagined he was living off Red Bull.

'What do you think's wrong then?' Theo asked Doctor Redhill.

'Like I said, the tests we carry out are pretty rudimentary. They can only tell us so much, but we're going to refer you to the on-call neurology team. Your reflexes are a bit too dull for our liking and that might be connected to why you've fallen and been having problems. They'll be able to ascertain what's going on with more clarification. The good news is your cruciate ligaments are intact. Right, let's check how those ribs are doing. Are you okay if I examine them?'

Theo removed his top and lifted his arms and did everything else that the doctor asked him to. He'd gone into autopilot because inside he was screaming: *Neurology! What the hell do I need to see neurology for?*

'We'll get a chest X-ray done just to check your ribs, but

otherwise you've come off lightly. Could have been a lot worse. I'll get the X-ray booked in and I'll call the on-call team. I can't guarantee when either of those will happen, but hopefully you won't be waiting more than a few hours.'

Theo put his top back on after the doctor had departed. He wanted to hide under a rock, but having his shirt on was as good as it was going to get.

'I'm going to get us some lunch if we're going to be here that long.'

'You don't have to wait with me, Owen. You can get back to work and I'll get a taxi home.'

'Do you really think I'd be able to concentrate on work knowing you're waiting here? They might have cleared your spine, but I'm not leaving until they make me.'

Theo shrugged before realising he shouldn't do that because it hurt. 'Thank you for the support. It's much appreciated.'

'What do you want from the canteen?'

'I've heard their pie is particularly good.'

'I'll see what I can do and, mate, don't go googling anything while you wait. It'll only make you panic more.'

Theo appreciated having a close enough friendship that Owen knew that's where his mind was at. Blind panic because he didn't know what to expect.

'Can I ask you a favour?'

'What's that?' Owen asked.

'Can we keep this between us for now? I don't want to worry anyone, especially Kate.'

He should probably tell his new girlfriend first, but Kate had been through enough recently.

Theo and Owen both knew this wasn't nothing. It would be an X-ray and home if that was the case. But Owen nodded his agreement and Theo knew he wouldn't tell anyone. Theo just had to hold onto the hope there wouldn't be anything to tell.

CHAPTER THIRTY-ONE

KATE

Kate had the evening to herself for a change. In a way she was glad, because she knew there was a void in her life and Theo had filled it. But now she had some time to think about her brother and how much she missed him, which was welcome.

She'd not actively sought for Theo to fill the hole in her heart, but it had been a natural progression. Not seeing him for longer than twenty-four hours was giving her a chance to think about the next stage of her life. It was giving her a chance to note the changes and decide what she wanted to do about them.

Having been on a zero-hours contract since she qualified as a nurse, now was the time to apply for some guaranteed work time. Fortunately, there wasn't a shortage of jobs to apply for. A shortage of nurses, yes, but right now that was in her favour. She'd applied for a job on the ward she was based on currently and obviously that was the one she was hoping to get, but she had submitted applications to three other wards in the hospital as well. It seemed wise to explore possibilities and, because of that, she was also looking at the available options at other hospitals within the county. In theory, she could spread her wings to wherever she wanted. She could look for vacancies in Scotland, or even explore the possibility of work in Australia. The world was her oyster as the expression went.

Even though that was the case, she didn't plan on making any drastic changes. She loved the ward she worked on and the staff she worked with, some of whom were also her housemates. She needed to keep some of the staples in her life just as they were. She also didn't want to abandon her parents off the back of her brother's death. They were adjusting to losing one child. They didn't need the other to take flight quite so dramatically.

In the end, Kate applied for two other jobs outside of the hospital she knew like the back of her hand.

Once she switched her laptop off, she was glad to find Freya in the lounge area of the house they shared. Often, when she was home, her housemates were all working shifts or recovering from them.

'How are you doing? Do you want a hot drink?' Freya asked.

Kate knew another cup of tea wasn't what she needed. 'What I'd really love is something stronger!'

'Let's do that then. We need a catch-up, it feels like it's been ages.'

It wasn't long before they were both ready and out the door, heading towards the local pub.

'I still feel rubbish about missing Lauren's wedding.' It had taken place the same week that Matthew had passed away, and going hadn't been a possibility for Kate.

'You know she completely understands. You had to be there for your brother. Nobody is holding any grudges or anything like that.'

'I know. But it's hard to shrug off the guilt of missing something so important for such a good friend. Are they back from their honeymoon yet?'

'A few days ago, but she won't be back to work until Wednesday. The rota worked in her favour.'

'I'll message her. Try and see if we can arrange to meet up.'

Freya purchased a bottle of rosé wine for them to share and they went outside to enjoy it in the sunshine.

'So tell me about Theo. I've only heard whispers, so I want a first-hand account!'

'Tell me the whispers you've heard, and I'll tell you if they're true?' Kate hadn't realised quite how much she'd cut herself off from her usual social circle. It hadn't been intentional as she'd needed the time to come to terms with losing Matthew. It just so happened that Theo had featured rather heavily in her recovery.

'I heard something about a romantic dinner in the canteen! Apart from that, I only know that you met him on the way back from the hen do and that, after Matthew requested it, he's been a fairly major part of your life since. Obviously, some of that might be hearsay, but I thought you needed some time rather than getting quizzed.'

'You've got the main elements correct. And thank you for not probing before now. Not that I would have minded, but you're right about needing some time to come to terms with losing Matthew.'

They took a seat on the nearest picnic bench and Freya set about pouring them both a glass of wine.

'So, how are you doing? On both fronts that is. Losing your brother and finding a new man. I feel like we've got a lot to catch up on.'

'You need to fill me in with what you've been up to as well.'

'I've been working and not much else. That's why I'm relying on you for the conversation.'

Kate took a sip of her wine before starting. She needed to wet her whistle before going into anything in depth.

'Losing Matthew has been hard, but we're lucky. We had time to make decisions and prepare ourselves. I know it sounds clichéd, but in many ways, I think I'd done some of my mourning already. I'm not saying it hasn't hurt because it has, but Theo has softened the blow.'

'Has he now? Tell me everything.'

Freya said it in such a way that it sounded like she wanted measurements to be included.

'I'd describe it as being delightfully unexpected. I would never have even considered starting to see someone, but my brother had other ideas. He's the reason I saw him as soon as I did because he wanted to meet Theo. After that, we just clicked, and it's felt a bit like a whirlwind romance since that point.'

'And where's the *gorgeous* Theo tonight? Why isn't he joining us?'

Kate drank some of her wine, discovering that she'd finished off the best part of a glass already.

'He's working late. He's making up for some of the time he's missed. Theo's a workaholic at heart.'

'What about you? How's it been returning to work?'

'It's been cathartic really. I thought being back at the hospital might only make me think of my brother, but he's part of the reason I became a nurse so instead I found it was nice being back.' Kate necked the last of her wine as Freya set to refilling both their glasses. '*And* I've started to apply for full-time jobs, with my first choice being D4, of course. It's been great having the ability to be zero hours and allow my job to fit around caring for Matthew, but it's time I got some more solid nursing hours.'

'That's *great* news, Kate! Where else have you applied to?'

Kate listed all the wards and hospitals she'd applied to earlier that day. It was nice to have things in her life that she was excited about again. A new boyfriend. Hopefully a new job before long. An endless list of possibilities.

And however much she missed her brother, there was a

relief in knowing he was free. Because she had a sense of beginning to unfurl her wings towards an unfamiliar freedom as well.

CHAPTER THIRTY-TWO

KATE

Having made the first steps in applying for permanent nursing hours, there was one person Kate wanted to tell above all others.

With Matthew now gone, that person had become Theo.

In a short space of time, he'd become her world and she found he was the one she wanted to share life events with the most.

Only he hadn't replied to her text message.

She'd not heard from him on WhatsApp.

And he'd not been answering her calls.

It was the longest they'd been out of touch with each other and she was starting to get worried. She didn't want that to continue throughout another shift so she was going to try again.

'Hi! Are you there? I was beginning to worry.' Kate was surprised at the call being answered.

'Hi, sorry! I've been really caught up with this new project at work. How are you?'

'I'm okay. I've been applying for more permanent hours. I've already got an interview through for next week.'

'That's amazing! Which ward is it for?'

'One of the elderly care wards. I've applied to the ward that

I've been working on and that'll be my first choice, but I'll have to wait and see what happens.'

'Great! That's really great.' The tone of Theo's voice didn't hold any enthusiasm. It was like talking to someone she hadn't spent the past month falling in love with.

'So, tell me more about this project?' she asked, wondering what was distracting his attention.

'It came in this week and it's an unusual one for us. It's a playground project. Something we've never done before. We always like new challenges so we decided to go in together to do the pitch. In fact, Owen's coming over this evening to discuss it further.'

'That sounds like a fun project.' She tried not to allow any disappointment to come across. She was hoping she'd be the one discussing her job applications with him, cosied up with a takeaway.

'I'm not sure it is when you have a go on some play equipment and end up falling off. I've got a considerable amount of bruises as a result, so I'm resting up a bit this week. Shall we sort something out for the weekend?'

'Really? Why didn't you say?'

'I didn't want to worry you. We got it checked out and I haven't broken anything, but I am taking some time for R&R. Hopefully by the weekend I'll feel less delicate and we'll have this project underway.'

As they sorted details over what to do and when, Kate came away from the call rather deflated. She'd quickly become used to Theo being a solid part of her life. It was as if she had a Parker Knoll chair in the corner of the room and she'd gone to sit on it, only for the legs to fall off. It was at odds to what she'd become used to. It was enough to make her worry, even if it was only because they'd been living in each other's pockets and she hadn't expected that to change.

CHAPTER THIRTY-THREE

KATE

Kate had butterflies in her stomach like she'd never had before with Theo. There had always been a natural canter to their time together, she'd never felt like she had to fuss or worry.

But today, she was doing all of those things. Concerning herself over what to wear and what to say.

They were meeting at an Italian restaurant. That in itself was unusual. Theo normally offered to give her a lift, but today he'd said he wanted a drink, so Owen had offered to be their taxi later in the evening.

Rather than waiting in the cold given it had started raining, Kate went to the table solo with only breadsticks for company for the first twenty minutes. Theo being late was something else that had never happened. Another thing giving her cause to worry in a way she hadn't previously. It was hard to know how to let it sit. Was it just that the first flush was over now and other things in life were bound to take priority?

When Theo did appear, Kate couldn't help but gasp. Along the side of his face was a purple bruise as if he'd been in a fight. There was also a mark on his neck that ran lower than his collar. It made her wonder how many others there were.

'Oh my God! You never told me you'd hurt yourself that badly.' Kate rushed up to get a closer look, but Theo practically flinched in obvious pain.

'I know. I didn't want to worry you. It was just a silly tumble. I didn't break anything, so it looks far worse than it is.'

'But you've hurt yourself? How did you do it?' Kate took a seat again, trying to take in his injuries from afar. 'When you said you'd fallen off some play equipment, I'd imagined a bruised elbow. Not a full-on face plant.'

Theo gingerly took the seat opposite. 'Owen and I thought it would be a good idea to visit some of the local play parks. We did it after work and by the time we'd been to several it was beginning to get dark. Because there weren't any children about, we'd allowed our inner child to come out to play. I took a spectacular tumble from the monkey bars. Landed really awkwardly. Turns out that I might have an inner child, but my outer child no longer has the same reaction speeds.'

'How many bruises have you got?' It wasn't just the bruises making Theo look different. He seemed paler somehow. As if all the blood cells were busy repairing the knock he'd taken.

'Several. You can count them later if you like, but that'll be as exciting as it gets until they've healed some more.'

'I'm just glad you didn't break anything. Are you okay?' Kate had to ask. There was an unease settling in her stomach over what had happened.

'I am okay, for the most part. I'll just be glad when I don't look like someone used me as a human pincushion and punchbag.'

They placed their order and Kate hoped he truly was okay. For a while, they'd had a spell weaved over them and it was as if it had taken a holiday. Or perhaps a knock, given that was exactly what had happened to Theo.

By the time they'd eaten and they were waiting for Owen to collect them, Kate was feeling decidedly happier. She'd read things into what was happening and made them into something else. Now they were together most of her concerns had washed away.

There was no question about whether she was going to spend the night at his flat. Not after they'd discussed his bruises and how she was allowed to examine them.

It was her first time meeting Owen. Other than shaking her hand, he didn't say much and just carried out his role of taxi driver. Kate guessed she'd have to try and win him over another day when she hadn't had a drink already.

'I'm going to apologise now as I'm going to take the stairs one at a time.'

'Did you hurt yourself that badly?'

'Like you wouldn't believe.'

Kate had packed a chemise in anticipation of the overnight stay. By the time she'd got changed in the bathroom, when she came out Theo was already out of his trousers and shirt with only his boxers remaining. He'd lain down on the bed, but she could tell he wasn't lying there in expectation.

When she looked over his bruises on his invitation, there weren't two of his joints that didn't have some kind of mark between them.

'What kind of play equipment was it? I hope the play-ground you design is a lot safer.' Kate sat on the side of the bed, next to Theo's side. She traced a few of the larger bruises with her finger and noted the grazes he also had.

'I thought I'd done my ribs in. We did get it checked over, before you worry.'

'I wish you'd told me.'

'I didn't want you to worry when it was just me being an idiot. Owen wasn't a klutz like me and didn't fall off, possibly because he didn't muck around as much as I did.'

'I'm not sure I can hug you. I don't know which parts to hold without hurting you.'

'It's okay. Switch the light off and come to bed and I can do the holding.'

Once the room was dark, Kate nestled into Theo's arms. Being wrapped in them was exactly what she needed. For a minute, she'd been worried that the honeymoon period she'd found herself in had started to lose its magic.

But here it was surrounding them as she fell asleep in Theo's arms. And that comfort allowed any concerns to float away as she relaxed into her dreams.

CHAPTER THIRTY-FOUR

THEO

Once again, Theo used work and the imaginary project as the reason for having to get up so early. It was only half an hour earlier than he normally left his flat, but he felt bad for feeding another lie into the piggy bank of them he seemed to be storing up.

Kate murmured something about applying for more jobs later and he kissed her forehead before leaving, even though she was still in a sleepy stupor. He wished he could stay there with her, but an appointment and hopefully some answers were waiting for him.

As was Owen.

He was glad not to be facing this entirely alone, but in some ways he wished he was. Especially as he knew what was coming next.

'Did you tell her then?'

'You know I haven't. I said I wasn't going to.'

'Don't you think she'll hate you for not mentioning it? You're going for a neurology appointment. That's pretty major.'

'Not if it's a trapped nerve. They did list that as one of the possibilities.'

'Among other things.'

'Look, Kate has been through a lot in a very short time. I don't want to add to that load. Can we concentrate on getting there? It might help if I know what I'm dealing with.'

'Okay, mate. It's your call.'

'It is. And the minute you ask Sharon out, that's when you can tell me what to do about my love life.'

Theo knew that his mentioning the company secretary would shut Owen up. It always did and it was a cheap move, but one that he'd resorted to before and probably would again. He didn't feel bad on this occasion, given that he'd already said he wouldn't be telling anyone anything until he had more of an idea as to what was going on. Owen knowing was all he needed right now.

Neither of them spoke again until they were out of the car and in the hospital asking a helpful volunteer for some directions.

It was odd, Theo had spent more time in this hospital recently, but because the place was so big and they were heading to an entirely different department, he didn't know where to go.

Once they knew it was an extension to the rear of the hospital, they got their bearings and started to head in the right direction.

'Are you okay?' Owen asked.

Theo knew he wasn't asking as a truce, not that there needed to be one. He was asking because Theo's foot had just scuffed against the lino. It wasn't the first time it had happened. And Theo hadn't wanted to admit it to himself that it was actually happening. He wanted it to be imagined. He wanted it to be down to an unevenness along the floor that wasn't obvious to the naked eye. At least that's what he'd managed to blame the first time it had happened with no one else about.

Now Owen had asked he knew it was none of those things. His foot scraped again as if to confirm it.

'I'm glad to be here.' It was all he was able to say for now. Because he wasn't okay, he knew that. It was the reason he was here.

'Theo Parrish, here to see Mr Welsh.'

The receptionist soon had him checked in and the wait that followed seemed to slow down time.

One minute became five.

For several of them, Theo considered leaving. If he left before the doctor even spoke to him, there was the opportunity to pretend none of this was happening. But, of course, that would be stupid given the fall that had resulted in this referral. Another fall landing differently might create a completely different outcome. A full stop of sorts.

'Thanks for taking the time off to be here,' Theo said to Owen. They might not agree on him not informing anyone else, not even his sister, but he was grateful to have his best friend by his side.

'Mr Parrish,' a nurse called.

'That's me.' Theo gave an awkward wave before making his way over.

'I'm Amanda. I just need to take all your observations before you go through to see the doctor.'

Theo followed all her instructions as she documented his height and weight, before going on to things like his blood pressure and temperature.

After that it was back to waiting. Owen had brought a book so was way more prepared than Theo was. Not that he'd be able to concentrate on the words if he did have one with him.

'That was quick!' Owen looked up from the pages he'd been staring at as Theo sat down again.

'They've only taken my blood pressure etcetera. I've got to wait again to see the doctor.'

About a chapter of Owen's book later, Theo was called in to see the consultant by the same nurse who'd taken his vitals. Owen gave him an encouraging smile and a pat on the back as he stood up.

'Mr Parrish, great to meet you. I'm Mr Welsh, one of the neurology consultants. Can you confirm your date of birth for me and then we'll go through your history.'

Theo provided all the information the consultant required up until the point he'd found himself at the bottom of a stairwell.

'Has there been anything else that's caused a problem? Any other symptoms?'

Theo thought about the new scuffing habit his foot had developed.

'In the last week, sometimes my foot has scraped the floor.'

'And is there any family medical history to be aware of? Any strokes or heart attacks?'

Mr Welsh proceeded to list a number of medical conditions and, after mentioning his father's heart attacks, it was a 'no' for each of them. More in-depth questions followed including questions about the countries he'd travelled to and whether he'd ever had any STDs and whether he'd been tested recently.

Theo wasn't entirely sure what any of those would have to do with a dodgy knee that had given way, but as he was beginning to sense it was like an episode of *House*, he answered dutifully.

'Right, I'm going to give you a full MOT of your body. I'm going to test all of your reflexes and see if I agree with the findings from the other doctors.'

'What did they find?' Theo asked.

'Only that some of your reflexes seemed to be duller than they would have liked. I just need to check if they were correct and we'll go from there.'

Theo decided not to ask any more questions after that. He

realised they couldn't give any kind of one hundred per cent accurate answer yet, so there was no point in asking. They'd tell him once they knew.

Over the next few minutes, Theo had to strip down to his boxers and get into various positions so the consultant was able to check his reflexes. Ones he didn't even know existed.

'Right, if you want to put your clothes back on and we'll discuss next steps.'

For a moment, Theo considered staying in his boxers forever. That way he didn't have to face whatever the next steps were. Sadly, he was feeling too cold to stage any kind of protest. Being prodded and poked with various instruments had given him goosebumps. Ones that were chilling him to his core.

Once he was dressed it took all his mental energy to return to the chair to listen to what Mr Welsh had to say.

'As suspected, we're going to have to do various additional tests to pinpoint what's causing these issues. We need to do some blood tests, an MRI and some electrophysiological tests and some nerve conduction studies.'

'That sounds like a lot. Are they necessary?'

'Each of the tests look at different factors that will help us come to a conclusion. So, yes, they are all required to give us a full picture. The blood tests can be arranged now and you can have them before you leave today. The other tests will be a separate appointment, which you'll get in the post over the next couple of days. I'll make sure they're a priority so they'll be done within the next fortnight.'

'What are you expecting to find?' Theo knew he'd promised himself that he'd stop asking, but he wanted to have some idea of what he was facing.

'At some point along your nerve, the communication path is being disrupted. We know that's happening, but right now we don't know why. It might be that the nerve is trapped, or it might be something like there's damage to the myelin sheath which can be caused by a few conditions. Until we've had a deeper look into things, we won't have a clear answer. We'll get everything booked up and I'll see you again once we have all that information. Is that clear?'

Theo didn't answer. He didn't know if not having any answers yet made anything clear.

'Do you have any questions?'

'No,' Theo whispered.

'Whatever it comes back as we'll put in all the resources needed, so try not to worry.'

Of course, Theo did nothing but worry.

For the entire time he was with Owen on the return to his flat.

For every day and night until the appointments came through the post.

Every time he deferred seeing Kate, knowing he didn't want to drag her into this.

Even when he lay in bed at night.

Something was wrong, he knew that. And his instincts told him it wasn't going to be an easy fix when he did finally get his answers.

CHAPTER THIRTY-FIVE

KATE

Kate was doing her utmost to concentrate on herself. She'd not seen Theo for over a week and the project he was working on seemed to be taking over everything else. It was leaving a hollow feeling after they'd spent the evening in each other's arms and she'd thought they were back on track.

She was doing her best to ignore any concerns she had about their relationship because today she had two interviews. One for the care of the elderly ward which was the first she'd received. The second was for D4, the ward she had been working on since she qualified. The ward sister had caught wind of the fact she'd also applied elsewhere so eagerly set up an interview date.

Kate was waiting outside the first interview room. It was weird to be in the hospital and not be in a nurse's uniform. Not that she'd worn that all the time when she'd been at her brother's bedside, but a lot of the time she'd visited him in scrubs. So to be in smart clothes with her Continuous Professional Development folder in her hands seemed at odds to how things were usually.

Right now, she was wracked with nerves to the point that parts of her were trembling slightly.

She stood up and paced a little, trying to distract herself. This was only the warm-up interview. The one that she wasn't worried too much as to whether she got it or not.

She glanced at her phone and still *nothing*. She would have thought Theo would have sent a good luck message, or something. Some signal that he'd read her last two messages, but there hadn't been anything. She really didn't want a man – or rather the lack of hearing from him – to be contributing to her nerves.

Once she was called into the interview and she had to concentrate on the questions the shaking started to settle down. They were giving her certain scenarios and asking what she would do in them, along with various other questions aiming to highlight her strengths and weaknesses. She liked to think she didn't have any weaknesses. Although, she knew she had a big one currently... *Theo*. Not that that was a suitable answer for what they were looking for.

Instead, she managed to come up with answers like being too caring. Negatives that could also be viewed as positives. At the end, Kate was given some observation charts to analyse and state what she'd do with each of the patients they represented. As the issues within their charts were either obvious or the patient history gave telltale signs of the answers they'd be looking for, Kate came away happy with how it had gone. They said she'd know by the end of the week, and she knew if she was offered the position, and not the one she was hoping for, she would take it.

There were two hours in between the interviews. To kill some time and to make use of the sample body sprays, Kate headed down to the small row of shops not far from the hospital. She knew she'd sweated more than she'd like to and wanted to make sure she didn't stink for the next interview. There wasn't enough time to wait for the bus and head back to the flat so this was a good back-up plan.

It was just as she'd spritzed her wrists with some sample perfume that she saw Owen. He was gathering lunch items to put together a meal deal. He was two rows away, but there was no mistaking it was him.

Kate hesitated. She'd only met him once and she didn't know what to do or say, but she felt compelled to act somehow. If nothing else, it might help give her a clearer head for her next interview for the job that she wanted. That seemed like an important enough reason and it was an opportunity she didn't want to miss.

As Owen went to queue, Kate made sure she was behind him.

'Oh, it's Owen, isn't it?' Kate said, trying to make sure it sounded like chance rather than a deliberate move.

Owen turned with his eyes bulging out of his head momentarily. 'Um, yes, Kate. How are you?'

'One interview down. One to go.'

'Good luck with those.'

'Have you seen Theo today? He's not been returning my messages.' Kate had already worked out that Owen had hold of two meal deals. He was either very hungry or with someone.

'Hasn't he? I'll speak to him, but he's been off with the flu.' Owen shifted from one foot to the other as if he now had hot coals underneath him.

'Really? I thought he would have said something. What are you doing so close to the hospital by the way?' For some reason, his change in demeanour made Kate wonder if he was being truthful. Not that she knew him well enough to suss that out with any clarity.

'I'm about to visit one of our projects. It isn't far from here. My secretary is with me, so I thought I'd better shout her some lunch.' Owen smiled, but it was as robotic as they got.

As soon as a self-service checkout was free, Owen made a beeline for it.

Kate didn't know what to do. She felt hollow. The stress of the interviews and knowing that whatever she'd had with Theo seemed to be disintegrating, while still in the shadow of losing her brother was making her want to cry right in the middle of the shop floor. Instead of giving in to the waiting tears, Kate marched over to Owen.

'I'm going to take a guess the food is actually for Theo. In which case, when you get back to him, can you ask him to call or message or something?' Kate failed to add, *preferably in the next hour so I can give my interview one hundred per cent focus.*

'I'll make sure I speak to him.' Owen practically hot-footed it out of the shop.

Kate was tempted to follow him. She knew the chances were that he was with Theo. That way she wouldn't have to sit around waiting for a phone call like a fool. However tempting it was, she knew preparing for her interview was more important and she decided she should get some lunch as well. Even though she wasn't sure she had the stomach for it, she didn't want to regret not having some later. She knew she'd feel better for eating.

As she was sitting in the nearby park, trying to quell her nerves, she stared at her phone waiting for some kind of response. Nothing came from Theo. But messages from her parents and Freya arrived.

Those messages settled her slightly. They helped her to concentrate on giving the best interview she'd ever given. The whole time she thought of her brother, Matthew. Of how much of a blessing he'd give to this move in her life. This ward had given her so much flexibility in allowing her to care for him and now she wanted to return that kindness by fulfilling the hours she'd always wanted to.

She went in with the confidence of someone who was going

to smash it and knowing all of the interview panel made her relax more than in the previous interview.

After Kate had answered another series of questions, the ward sister said, 'We'll be in touch soon.'

Kate hoped she wouldn't be waiting for long. She didn't want to put any bets on whether she'd hear from Theo or find out if she got the job first.

With an increasingly heavy heart, she figured the odds were better for the latter.

CHAPTER THIRTY-SIX

KATE

'Soon' turned out to be the same day on the job offer front. Before she'd got home, she'd had the call from D4 ward and she'd happily accepted and it wasn't long before Freya had her out to celebrate.

'Another for the excellent news!' Freya declared as she placed another cocktail in front of Kate.

'What's this one?' Kate knew she should stop. This many cocktails were a recipe for disaster.

'Not sure. Something like sex on the beach or a frolic in a forest. They've made sure they're all rude like some kind of gimmick.'

'It's working, though, if we're buying them all!'

'True. True. At least our cocktails are making us feel lucky.'

'We are lucky. Just not in that department.' Kate had told Freya about everything that had happened with Theo over the last fortnight. Or rather, the things that hadn't happened. It was beginning to feel like the never-ending saga of being ignored. Only Theo kept throwing bones. He wasn't feeling well enough to celebrate tonight, but they'd do something special soon.

She wouldn't have minded so much if it didn't feel like a

complete contrast to the beginning of the relationship when they hadn't been able to get enough of each other.

'I think I need to do something that'll be make or break,' Kate concluded.

'Like what?'

'I'm thinking I should give him a date and time and see if he turns up.'

'Oh, Kate... He'd be a fool if he didn't.'

'I know. And I really hope he does. I know he's had a fall, but I'm a nurse. Illness is kind of my speciality. But he's keeping me at arm's length. It's been like night and day.'

'Some people, especially men I've found, aren't great at being looked after. They much prefer to get through any ailments solo. I'm not sure why, but hopefully it's just that. What date and time are you going to give him?'

'I don't want an audience if that's what you're planning.' Kate took a sip of the vibrant yellow cocktail and gave an immediate apology to her liver on tasting how strong it was.

'No, not at all. I'm just intrigued about what your plan is.'

Kate hadn't thought about it at length given she'd only just decided it was a good idea. Of course, that might be the influence of the alcohol, but she wanted the relationship they'd had. Not whatever was going on now.

'I think I'm going to book a weekend away and get him to meet me at the train station. If he doesn't show, then I've still got a weekend away to look forward to.'

'Is that sensible?'

'A weekend away was the first thing we ever did together. If he's been poorly, a restful break away will do him some good. It's go big or go home. I don't want to carry on believing I've met the love of my life and then find out it was all an illusion. That's what it feels like at the moment. That perhaps he felt obliged to be a part of my life because of everything that was happening with my brother.'

'I've only met him briefly and didn't get that impression, but we both know he's been acting strangely and we've both had our fair share of men acting strangely. So, I think you're right to see if it's do or die. I don't want anyone messing you about.'

'Me neither.'

Now Kate had said it out loud, she knew coming up with a plan was the right thing to do. She didn't want to spend her days filling in the blanks as to what was going on. The contrast was too great to not highlight that all was not well.

Even though she was far too inebriated, once they were home, Kate put her laptop on to turn her thoughts into an actual plan.

She decided to make it a trip to Southfern train station where they'd first met and booked at a nearby bed and breakfast. It would give them a chance to rekindle some of the highlights of that first month. It seemed like a great idea in her current stupor.

She'd message him in the morning with the details. And hope that he'd say yes. Because if he didn't, she didn't want to remain in this strange limbo that they seemed to be in.

The next day, Kate waited until the celebration hangover had dissipated. Once that had gone and it still seemed like a good idea, she decided to send the message she'd formulated the night before.

Dear Theo,

I feel like we need to reconnect. A lot has happened in the time we've known each other, and as you've been unwell, I thought we could do with a weekend away together. A chance to recover and reset. It's already booked and it's my

THE DAY HE DISAPPEARED   169

treat this time. Meet me at the train station at 18:30 on Friday
and it'll be my turn to whisk you away.

Sending love, Kate xx

Kate had never mentioned the 'L' word in any previous
context with Theo. She didn't know why she was breathing life
to that now. It was probably because she'd been harbouring
those feelings from the start and she wanted him to know it was
there.

But there was no answer.

No acknowledgement about being asked.

No indication either way as to whether he'd be there.

Later in the day when she was offered a last-minute night-
shift because of some unexpected sickness, Kate jumped at the
chance. She doubted she'd be able to sleep anyway while staring
at her mobile. At least when she was on a shift, she left her
mobile phone in her locker and ignored it because she was too
busy concentrating on caring for her patients.

The first part of the shift was busy. Getting everyone ready
for bed, cleaning and changing where necessary. Doing the
meds round and making sure everyone was ready for lights out.

Not that it was full-on lights out like they would be at home.
The night light setting allowed Kate to see well enough to navigate the ward.

After midnight, the shift went much slower. When she
went on her break, she'd normally check her phone, but tonight
she was going to ignore it. She very much doubted anything
would have changed since putting it away. She managed to wolf
down the sandwich she'd brought and lay down in the on-call
room to try and get half an hour of kip. Normally, she'd have
had a sleep in the day to prepare, but as she hadn't had much
notice, this would help her through the remainder of the shift.

She hadn't been in the room since Matthew had died. The

smell inside – a kind of clinical mustiness – instantly brought her back to those days of waiting. Of knowing the end was near and that she didn't want to miss it after coming so close to that happening.

Pulling the thin blanket over her, Kate breathed in the mustiness. She liked that it reminded her of Matthew. She was thankful for this place and the people here that had supported her during one of the most difficult times.

She tried not to think too much about Theo, who'd also been there for her. Perhaps he was only ever meant to be a fleeting gift. A person that passed through her life at the moment they were most needed, but it would turn out it was never a permanent thing.

But she fell asleep thinking about him. Finding both Theo and Matthew dominating her dreams until the alarm clock she'd set woke her from her power nap.

It hadn't been as refreshing as it normally was and when the lead on the shift asked if she'd be able to do the following night as well, she said yes.

She'd be able to spend the day sleeping, numb to the fact the man of her dreams seemed to be beyond her grasp.

CHAPTER THIRTY-SEVEN

THEO

When Owen asked how Theo was feeling, he skipped several parts of the answer. He didn't tell Owen that he hadn't slept a wink. He didn't mention that he'd thrown up before leaving the flat as the anticipation of knowing had got too much. He didn't mention any of the micro concerns his body was currently giving him. He gave the classic response of 'fine' even though he was anything but.

The turmoil of the past week had seen him telling white lies to everyone he loved. His entire family thought he had the flu, but really he'd been heading back and forth to the hospital for test after test. He'd kept communication with Kate to a minimum, using an imaginary project as his continued excuse.

Hopefully he was at the end of having to fill in this strange period of not knowing. Because today was different. Today, he hoped, would contain answers.

Owen didn't press him further. They both knew there were no words until he heard the ones he needed to know. And he knew they wouldn't be good ones. His body had given enough signals as to something being out of kilter.

'Do you both want to come through?' the nurse asked after they'd taken a seat in the waiting area.

It was unnerving that she didn't even have to call his name to know that's who they were waiting for.

Theo and Owen exchanged an awkward glance.

'We're not partners,' he said, obviously wondering if that's what had been assumed.

'I just thought you might want your friend in for support.'

Support.

The thought that he needed support made the floor open up like a cavern. One he wished he could hide in.

'I'll come in, mate. If you're happy for me to?'

'What if I end up crying?'

'Wouldn't be the first time I've seen that happen.'

Theo nodded.

Owen tapped his knee. 'You could do far worse than me, you know.'

His best friend's attempt at humour was almost enough to put a smile on his face, but that was never going to happen. Not right now. He realised he wanted Kate here, but he had no desire to put her through the worries he and his best friend were sharing now.

Once they were seated in the room, Theo knew it was going to be bad news. There was a morbid tension in the atmosphere, and it was written there in both the doctor's and nurse's expressions.

Theo tried to zone out for a minute. He pretended they were here to discuss a new extension for the hospital so he and Owen were really here to do a pitch.

'Having conducted all our tests, we think what we're seeing here are the early signs of motor neurone disease.'

'No!' Theo heard himself saying out loud. 'It's my *ligaments*,' he said, shaking his head and holding it in his hands as he did. Of all the conditions that he'd been reading about – even though Owen had told him not to – that was the one he'd been hoping not to hear.

'I'm afraid it is. I know the early indications being unilateral might have led you to thinking it was other issues, but MND can present in many ways and affects different parts of the body.'

'What treatment is there?' Owen asked, at least one of them hadn't gone into shock and was thinking about the facts.

'MND is a progressive situation. There is no cure as such, but we'll support and manage your symptoms and make sure you get all the help you need.'

'How long?' Theo's throat was so closed it was hard to get the question out.

'That's an impossible question to answer for you specifical-ly,' the doctor said with a kind smile. 'But I can tell you in very general terms. From diagnosis, it can be anywhere between one to five years with ten per cent living over ten years. We won't ever be able to pinpoint it exactly, but we can make sure that you're supported at every stage.'

Theo's throat fully closed at that point. Perhaps if he stopped breathing it wouldn't hurt as much. Perhaps if he blacked out from temporary lack of oxygen he'd forget what he'd just been told.

'Shit, mate. I never dreamed it would be something like that,' Owen said. 'Sorry for the swearing, Doc, it's just such a shock.'

'It's a lot to take in. Are you okay, Theo? Would you like us to get you a drink?'

Theo nodded. He suddenly had a thirst like he'd never known.

'Shall I make a tea? I'll get one for you as well,' the nurse said to them both, before heading out of the room.

'I know you will have lots of questions, so we'll make

another appointment before you go and we'll do regular check-ups with you.'

'Will it affect everything?'

'It will gradually result in your muscles not responding. You'll lose some movement and eventually it will affect things like your speech and ability to swallow. We'll keep an eye on everything and assist at every stage.'

The tea couldn't come quick enough and between them, Theo and Owen managed to come up with a barrage of questions for the doctor. What were the next steps? Were there any treatments that slowed the progression down? Would it follow a particular pattern?

They were all questions without the positive responses they were hoping for. The forecast held nothing but cloudy skies.

Theo had sensed it would be bad news. But this had ripped the carpet from underneath him and as he was already having trouble with his walking, he didn't know how he'd manage to get through this.

The only thing he did know for certain was that he couldn't put Kate through this. Not when life had already been crueller to her than she deserved.

CHAPTER THIRTY-EIGHT

KATE

By the time Kate reached the train station, she was running on forty-eight hours with no sleep. She'd done the two last-minute night shifts, but during the daytime when she should have been catching up, she'd been too overtired to sleep. It was the anxiety of not knowing whether Theo would turn up and as he hadn't yet replied, it was hard to guess.

It was such a contrast to how things had been between them that she wasn't sure what to think. She should be full of buoyant cheer as she headed off for her second weekend away with her new boyfriend, only this time it wasn't in the wake of her brother's death. Only how could she be buoyant when she didn't know why he was acting so differently? The first flush of romance was no longer there and she had every expectation that she was going to be stood up. He'd ghosted her for over a week now, so it was a strong possibility.

There was a window of half an hour between the train setting off and the time she'd given Theo to arrive. She'd purchased her ticket already, but as she'd had no communication at all from Theo, she'd decided that getting his could wait.

And wait she did.

Until the time he was supposed to arrive.

Then five minutes after he was supposed to arrive.

The only thing keeping her from watching every single person entering the station were the messages from Freya demanding regular updates.

Is he there yet?

And now?

Does he know what he's missing?

Nearly all of Kate's answers were no. A steady stream of them as she came closer to accepting he wasn't coming.

He's an idiot.

Kate's fingers were about to tap out a singular yes in agreement.

'Kate?'

It was Theo's voice, but it sounded uncertain. As if he didn't recognise her, even from this distance, and needed her to confirm.

Glancing up she found herself laced with uncertainty. Theo looked washed out in a grey tracksuit, and he seemed to have lost weight since the last time she'd seen him.

'Are you okay?' she asked, more worried about how he was over anything else. She wasn't looking at the same man she'd met at the train station all those weeks ago.

'I'm fine, but...'

Theo didn't finish his sentence, but Kate managed to fill in some of the blanks.

He wasn't coming.

She'd been too busy taking in his appearance to realise the

obvious error. He didn't have a bag with him. No kind of luggage in his possession. He'd come here with no intention of coming with her.

'You're not coming.' Kate said it for him seeing as he'd gone mute.

'I'm not and I think it's time we called things off.'

Kate glanced around the station as if there might be a camera crew and she was about to discover she was being pranked.

'Why?' Her voice was loaded with emotion that she was too tired to try and hide.

Theo also glanced around the station, unable to look Kate in the eye. 'I made a promise that I don't want to break.'

Kate's face creased in confusion. 'Who have you made a promise to?' It certainly wasn't her.

'I made a promise to your brother to never break your heart. And I'm not going to be the kind of boyfriend you deserve. So, to stop that from happening, I'm calling it off. I'm sorry.'

Kate gulped air for a while as if she were a fish out of water. She didn't understand. 'But we were so good together. I thought you had the flu and a fall and this was just a short hiatus...'

Theo looked up to the station ceiling as if trying to draw strength from another realm. 'I'm sorry. It's nothing personal. I just don't want to hurt you.'

But Kate was already hurting. As if the past few months were bundling themselves up together to come and run her over. 'Have you met someone else?' she gasped. She wasn't sure why she was asking, but it felt as if there had to be an identifying factor in why this was happening.

'Nothing like that. Like I said, I'm keeping a promise not to hurt you. I'm sorry this is how it has to be. Take care of yourself, Kate.' Theo swept her into a hug and momentarily embraced her so hard it was possible it would have crushed her if she wasn't crushed already.

After that, he walked away, without looking back. Instead, he placed his hands behind his neck as if he was bracing for impact.

Kate only had a few minutes to make a decision. Did she run after him to try and discover what it was that had changed? Or did she head to the platform to go and get the now waiting train?

It turned out to be an easy decision with self-preservation in mind. She headed for the train, faster than she probably needed to when it wasn't about to leave straightaway. But she needed to do that in order to find the perfect seat. She wanted to find a private space in a quiet carriage so no one else would hear her heart shatter.

Theo had said he'd made a promise to her brother about not breaking her heart, but that still didn't explain what had changed. And she wasn't sure what a promise to her brother had to do with anything. Especially as calling things off was doing exactly what he claimed to be trying to avoid.

A numbness started to take over her when the couple of tissues she'd had with her were crumpled and spent. Ironically, they were from the same packet of tissues that Theo had given her all those weeks ago. Whatever she'd hoped for in booking this weekend away, it had definitely been with the intention of healing whatever the rift was that had appeared. She'd thought there was a chance that would happen.

Instead, she was on Plan B. A weekend alone and she only hoped that the heartbreak would pave the way for sleep. Because that seemed like the only thing that might take the pain away.

CHAPTER THIRTY-NINE

THEO

Theo hated himself. He knew that he had to let Kate go. It was what he needed to do for the best, but that hadn't made it any easier. He loved her. And at this juncture, he was trying to keep the hurt to a minimum.

He shouldn't have hugged her. It had made it worse. But he'd wanted one final contact. A moment to remember the time they'd spent together.

He should have known that contact would leave him wanting more. It would have been *so* easy to get on the train. To leave all his concerns and everything he was facing behind. A bit like they'd done in the aftermath of Matthew's death. He might not have packed anything, but he would have been able to find what he'd need to get by easily enough. He could have erased his decision in a second.

But then the words Matthew had spoken to him came back to him with startling clarity.

Make sure to never hurt her in the way my death will.

At the time, it hadn't even occurred to Theo that he'd regret any such agreement, but he'd never known he'd be facing a similar destiny to Matthew.

And even without that promise, he couldn't allow Kate to go through it again. He didn't want to be the cause of that level of pain and even though he knew there would be some, because he was going through it too, it was better to do it now. It was better for him to be the bad guy and walk away.

But as he thought that, he also walked to the bridge over the railway. He knew she hadn't followed him, and he was glad. He wasn't sure he'd have been able to walk away a second time. Even if their trajectory was set for crash and burn, if she had followed him, he wasn't sure he'd have been strong enough to leave her again.

Instead, he watched from a spot where he knew he'd be able to see her without being seen.

She rushed onto the train and seeing her crying broke his heart, but that was nothing compared to what they'd face. That was something she'd already been through in this lifetime, no one deserved to face that twice. Not when there was a choice.

Even though Theo couldn't see where Kate was on the train, he remained there staring at it. There was time, if he hurried, to go and get the train. This didn't have to be how things ended. But he soon reminded himself this wasn't the fairy tale Kate deserved. He couldn't give her the future Matthew had wanted for her. And even without Matthew being part of their story, he still couldn't imagine wanting to put her through what he was facing.

The fleeting thought of joining the journey remained, but the other thing stopping him was the chance of falling again. Especially on another set of industrial stairs. His knee was already weaker. He'd bounced the first time, but he knew that luck wouldn't last.

Not that luck was with him. Not in any way. And as the train departed, Theo let the tears slide down his cheeks without interruption. As days went, the last two had been the worst in his life. He'd received a diagnosis that no one could ever be prepared for and he'd broken up with the love of his life, knowing that he needed to keep her from the heartache that would follow.

He might have remained there crying forever until he was made into a statue, but a small Yorkshire terrier sniffing his ankles pulled his attention away from the blank space he was staring into.

'Sorry, love,' the elderly lady owner said. 'Are you okay there?'

Theo rapidly wiped the tears away. 'I've just lost something... That's all.'

'Oh no! What is it? We'll help you look for it.'

The lady's white hair bobbed down as if they needed to look for a necklace or some other object.

'Sorry, I mean I've lost *somebody* and I don't think it'll ever be a simple case of finding her again.'

'Oh, love. Have you had your heart broken? You should get yourself home and make a hot cocoa. Your heart will heal, and there'll be other loves. You're still young. The world is your oyster.'

Theo offered his thanks without correcting her. She didn't need to know there wouldn't ever be another love. If he wasn't going to put Kate through it, he wasn't ever going to with anyone else. And she didn't need to know that the world wasn't his oyster. Not now his time was limited.

He didn't say any of those things. Instead, he got himself home knowing that a hot chocolate wasn't going to fix this evening. Because he was only at the beginning.

Breaking up with Kate to spare her had been the hardest thing he'd ever done. And he was filled with sadness knowing his own heart wouldn't ever have long enough to recover. He just had to hope hers did.

CHAPTER FORTY

THEO

Theo needed to summon up some courage because he'd called a family meeting at his grandparents' house for the following evening.

He didn't want to have to tell everyone the news on repeat. It would be torture. This method wouldn't be much better, but at least he'd be able to tell everyone at the same time.

Owen came with him. He was the emotional support buddy he never knew he'd need. They'd been friends since university, extending to them setting up their business together, but neither of them had realised what they were walking into the other day at the hospital. His friend hadn't left his side in that time, even providing a lift to the train station, and had been staying in the spare room at Theo's flat. He'd held Theo when he shed the expected tears over his decision about Kate. Perhaps he was worried what Theo might do so he was staying. Fortunately, nothing like that had crossed his mind. Instead, he was despairing at the unknown and mourning a necessary loss.

It was evening by the time they reached his grandparents' house and Owen had ordered a spread from a caterer as if they were here for a conference or board meeting. Perhaps they were. Perhaps that was how Theo should view it to distance himself away from knowing he was about to tell his family something about him that none of them would be able to make better.

Once they arrived, Owen also asked what everyone wanted to drink and set about making everyone what they needed, rather than leaving Theo's grandparents to it.

'This is nice,' his grandad said with a smile.

It broke Theo's heart to know that it wouldn't be that nice at all.

'Everyone take a seat,' Theo said once everyone was there and had a drink in hand.

'What's this all about?' his mum asked.

'Are you and Kate getting married already?' Anita joked.

'Nothing like that, I'm afraid.'

The room fell silent as his voice gave away they weren't there for any laughing matters. Suddenly, everyone realised that it was serious.

'Is everything okay, love?' Theo's nan asked.

Theo took a steadying breath, not that there was enough air in the world to make what he had to say next any easier.

'You all know that I've been having some trouble with my knee and I've been getting it looked into. Over the past few weeks it's been giving me considerably more trouble and at work, it gave way completely and I fell down the stairs.'

'Why didn't you tell us?' his sister asked.

'Let me finish. I didn't break anything, but when Owen took me to the hospital, they wanted to do more tests. They'd realised my reflexes weren't correct and that it must be connected. Yesterday, they were finally able to tell me what's going on and I'm afraid it isn't what I'd thought. It's actually motor neurone disease that's been causing me to have problems. Basically, my nerves and my muscles aren't talking to each other like they should and it's only going to progress. At the current time there is no cure.'

Theo's throat closed up again like it had in the hospital when he'd first been told. He'd wanted to say it all at once so it was out there, but he'd done it in such a rush it took a moment for anyone to react.

'But you are... What does that mean?' Anita asked.

Theo was still unable to talk, and he was incredibly thankful when Owen took over.

'It means that we're all going to need to support Theo as his needs adjust over the next few years. The doctor said he can't give us any kind of timescale, but the important thing is to make sure Theo's quality of life is the best that it can be.'

Various questions followed. Would Theo be able to drive still? Was his flat going to be the best place for him to be? What would happen about his job?

They were all things they were going to have to tackle over time, some more urgently than others.

'He can come and live with me,' Theo's mum offered.

'Or me,' Anita said.

'Or us,' his grandparents added.

'My suggestion would be that we use our expertise,' Owen said. 'If you're all happy to have Theo living with you, then I think we should visit each of your properties together and work out where would be best to build an independent ground floor fully accessible set-up for Theo. Obviously I'm on a fast forward with this idea, but knowing how long planning can take I figure it's best to come up with a futureproof solution.'

'What about Kate?' Anita asked. 'Is she going to live with you?'

Owen looked to Theo then. There were only so many questions he was able to field.

'We've called things off. I didn't think it was fair to put her through this given everything she's been through.' Theo's cheeks were wet with tears that he didn't have control over. He wiped some away with his sleeve.

'I'm sorry to hear that. I'm sorry to hear all of this.' It was Anita's turn to have her throat close, tears falling from her eyes as well.

One by one, Theo's family came and gave him a hug and whispered their reassurances. He knew this was going to be hard, but there was something comforting in knowing that everyone in the room was going to support him.

For a while silence followed before Theo's family muttered amongst themselves, discussing where would be the best place for the kind of accommodation they were talking about. Theo didn't join in. He was floating on a cloud somewhere unable to take part. It seemed impossible that this was his reality given he'd convinced himself some keyhole surgery would sort him out. And what had reached him wasn't the conversation that was going on now. It was what Owen had said earlier.

Over the next few years.

Few.

The word was floating in his head, its meaning too accurate to not hurt. It belonged in other sentences.

I'll just have a *few* more crisps.

It's only a *few* more days until my annual leave starts.

I've just got a *few* more steps to reach my count for the day.

Those were the kind of sentences that word belonged in. Not...

I've got a *few* more *years* left to *live*.

That shouldn't be possible and yet, that's why he was about to make plans to move so that he'd be cared for in the short future he now had.

It was the reason he'd had to end things with Kate. Because she deserved an entirely different future. One without the word *few* in it.

CHAPTER FORTY-ONE

KATE

To her surprise, when Kate arrived at the bed and breakfast, she'd fallen into an easy slumber. Apparently, exhaustion and heartbreak were the exact recipe needed for a long and deep sleep.

She woke with cracks of sunlight filtering into the room through the blind and for a while, she stayed in the cosy comfort of the white linen. She stared at the light refractions on the wall and listened to the seagulls' calls outside and convinced herself that this wasn't so bad.

Eventually she hauled herself out of bed, unable to resist the wafting smells of breakfast being cooked. She had thought she'd skip breakfast, but it turned out after not having dinner last night, she was ravenous.

After slipping on clothes, she checked her phone and immediately felt guilty because Freya had called and messaged her multiple times.

I'm okay. He turned up, but didn't come with me. I'll tell you more when you're awake and I'll phone you later.

Right now, she wanted to concentrate on the morning light and enjoying an English breakfast. Simple pleasures that she needed to embrace.

'Good morning,' the lady who ran the B&B chirped from the kitchen. 'Did you sleep okay?'

Kate hesitated in the kitchen doorway to speak to her. 'Like a baby.'

'Your friend is waiting for you in the dining room.'

Kate's face folded into confusion, while her stomach flickered with a tiny bud of hope. Was it Theo, after all?

'She got here late so she went straight to her room.'

She.

'Oh, thanks. I'll go find her.' She knew it had to be Freya.

'What are you doing here?' Kate asked as she found her at one of the quaint dining tables.

'You know *why* I'm here,' Freya said calmly, her chocolate-brown pixie haircut always looking perfect whatever the hour. 'And it's the reason I asked for all the details before you left. Just in case.'

Kate took her seat and helped herself to a piece of toast that was waiting in a rack and that Freya had already dived into.

'I've just read your message. Are you going to tell me what he said?'

On the one hand, Kate was delighted to see one of her best friends here to support her. On the other hand, she wanted to enjoy breakfast without having to mention the T word. She rather hoped she could have a weekend with him becoming known as he who must not be named.

'Okay, if I do, can we make it a one-time thing. I don't want to spend the weekend psychoanalysing what's happened.'

'Of course, I can understand that.'

'What made you turn up here?'

Freya spread some strawberry jam on another piece of toast.

They were going to be full before the main event arrived. 'Call it a gut feeling. When you told me about the plan, I thought it was a great idea to work out if this romance had any chance, but I had a feeling it wouldn't be the outcome we were hoping for. I rang to see if they had a spare room yesterday after you'd not had a response either way. And when you stopped responding, I figured it wasn't because Romeo had turned up and swept you off your feet.'

'You've got that right.' Kate spread generous amounts of butter on her toast as if it were the last meal she was going to have on earth. 'He did arrive, but not to come away with me like I'd hoped. He turned up to... to *dump* me.'

'*Really?* Did he tell you why?'

'No, not really. That part was in code. He told me he'd made a promise to my brother to never hurt me, so apparently ending it was to protect me from having my heart broken.'

'Did he really try and blame it on your brother? That's low.'

'My dead brother. Who I can't call to clarify if what he said was true.' Kate shook her head as if that would erase any negative thoughts. 'Theo seemed to think he was doing it out of kindness, but as he's not said why and called things off, I don't think I'll ever know. So if you work it out, do let me know. The mystery of the day he disappeared!' Kate knew she was putting on a brave face and trying to sound light-hearted, but, in truth, the only thing that had ever hurt more than this was losing Matthew.

'Here we are.' The B&B owner came to the table with two full plates of English breakfast. 'If you need anything extra, it's over with the buffet items. Enjoy!' She rushed out again as another couple arrived to have their breakfast.

'It really is his loss you know. Something obviously changed his mind, but he'll end up regretting it.'

'I don't know why, but I was always worried there was a chance that this would happen. That he'd perhaps felt obliged because of what was happening with Matthew and that he'd come to his senses. I'm glad really. I wouldn't want to remain with someone who felt trapped.'

'So, what were your plans if he didn't turn up?'

'What? Do you mean before one of my best friends arrived as a substitute?'

'Yes, what were your plans before *I* turned up?'

Kate started cutting into her bacon and egg, heartbreak not stopping her from wanting to eat. 'Honestly, I'm not sure I'd leave the confines of the B&B and the comfort of the bed. I might have ordered a pizza later in a real stupor of self-indulgence.'

'The bed was really comfortable. Well, how about we add a walk down to the beach seeing as we're so close. I imagine that's why most people book this place. Seems a shame to miss out on it.'

Kate nodded, while finishing a mouthful of food. 'Okay. It's a deal. As long as after we've finished this, I'm allowed to return to bed for at least an hour. And no more mentions of T.' She didn't want to say his whole name. 'Not until we're back home. This weekend was always going to be about moving on. Now I know in what direction, I just want to get my head round it at my own pace.'

'The only T I'm going to mention from now on is this type.' Freya lifted the teapot. 'Do you want one?'

'Yes, that's the only kind of tea I want to hear about.'

After they'd finished their breakfast feast, they managed to stick to their promise and Theo didn't get a mention for the rest of the weekend.

But Kate's heart missed him with every beat. She'd never thought of Theo as only being part of her life for a season. She'd thought she'd found her forever.

CHAPTER FORTY-TWO

THEO

Theo was standing in the middle of his grandparents' garden with Owen. He was finding the business of planning buildings entirely different with him as the main focus. Not least because this was never what he'd imagined his next step would be.

'We could relocate those rose bushes to the front?' his nan was saying.

Inwardly, Theo was grieving. He was grieving for the rose bush that might die while being transferred. He was grieving for his grandad's shed that would be flattened to make way for a one-storey annexe. He was grieving for his own plans where he'd seen his next step on the property market as a family home. He was grieving for the future with Kate that he'd started to daydream about. He was grieving for the train journey that he hadn't taken with her.

It was taking every inch of his usual glass half-full nature to keep smiling. Everything they were doing was to pool their best resources together. They'd settled on his grandparents' home as the best place to carry out their plan. It had the biggest garden space and several other properties along the same road had single level buildings in their gardens with various uses. Owen was volunteering his time, not only as the architect, but he was also going to project manage the build. Everyone had agreed it would work out well with his mum and sister coming to provide help, both to him and his grandparents as required. Theo was hopeful his grandparents would remain fit and active, and he could make the simple switch of converting the weekly shop to an online one. He was trying his hardest to see this as the best step forward, while aching for Kate to still be in the picture.

'Right, that's all the questions I needed to ask. I'll finish up the plans and as soon as possible I'll share them with you. We'd best head off.'

Theo said his goodbyes to his grandparents, ready to cross another thing off his long to-do list. This afternoon he had three lots of estate agents coming to his flat to give an appraisal ready to get the flat on the market. Its value had increased since he'd purchased it at the same time they'd started OT Architects. He'd wisely been making regular overpayments and now owned about eighty per cent of the property. Money that would fund the build at his grandparents'.

'Are you okay if I leave you to it?' Owen asked, once he'd delivered him to the flat.

'Of course.'

'I'll get on with the plan and send it over as soon as it's done. Are you going to be okay for the evening?'

'Yep. No plans here.'

'Give me a buzz if you need anything.'

'Will do. Thanks for everything.'

Theo was incredibly thankful for everything Owen was doing. But he didn't want his friend to think that he needed to be babysat. Even if there were times he was happy to have someone around, he wanted to enjoy time alone in his flat while he still had it. The flat buzzer ringing reminded him that wouldn't be for long.

'Come up,' Theo said, after pressing the button that allowed admittance. The video camera told him it was an estate agent. It was funny how they had a look about them that pointed to their profession.

'Are you happy for me to take pictures in case you do decide to list with us?'

'Yes, of course. Anything to save time.'

'Are you in a rush to sell?'

'Something like that.' Theo didn't wish to share the details of his recent diagnosis with strangers. He might have invited them into his home, but that didn't mean they got to learn what was going on with the fine print.

'Do you want to show me around?'

Theo nearly said 'if I have to', but decided acting like a sulking teenager wasn't going to help. The attitude that was almost making an appearance made Theo realise this wasn't something he wanted to be doing. It was the closing of another door to the life he thought he'd live.

'Follow me,' he said instead as they navigated the two bedrooms, bathroom, kitchen and living area.

It was when he opened the blind in the bathroom to improve the lighting that he noticed there were some products there that must belong to Kate. He never had got round to emptying a drawer for her, but he'd come across the occasional item that she'd left behind. He had to take a moment to remind himself why this was the plan now. That this was going to be better for everyone, none more so than Kate.

'It's a great flat with a clean aesthetic. The ones in this block don't come up very often so it should be a quick sale as we've got a waiting list for this kind of thing.'

'What do you think it's worth?' Theo attempted to shrug off the sentiment that had caught him by surprise and stuck to the practicalities. He listened to the figure with the build budget in mind and was pleased with the first evaluation. But he wasn't going to shake hands with the first agent. He was going to wait until he'd had the other evaluations before he decided.

The next two visits followed a similar pattern. Theo trying his best not to be hostile at the prospect of his new future, and the estate agents being overly eager for his business. He got it, as a business owner himself, but he ended up going with the one that hadn't asked intrusive questions in the hope that remained the case throughout. The flat would be on the market on Friday ready for the weekend, which according to the agent was one of the most popular times for searching for houses.

By the time evening came around, Theo ordered from his favourite takeaway that did a gym box kebab. It was all meat, salad and sauce and as those were his favourite parts it was a regular order. He especially liked that the delivery driver would always come up the stairs and bring it directly to his door. It was one less thing to worry about on the days that Theo's body didn't want to cooperate.

When it had been delivered and he'd started eating it, he couldn't help but feel sorry for himself.

It felt like a last supper. Soon this flat wouldn't be his. Its potential lost to a need. He couldn't help but think about Kate and wonder what she was up to. This weekend should have been theirs, but that was another thing where any potential had to be let go.

If she asked for the bathroom products back, he'd make sure he got them to her, but if not, he was going to keep them. If all he had to remind him of their relationship were whiffs of her shampoo, he'd take it.

Sad kebabs for one and sniffing his ex-girlfriend's shampoo were the way forward. There was another word that didn't belong in his life – ex. But he had to keep reminding himself why it had been essential. At least the food was good, even though nothing else in his life was.

CHAPTER FORTY-THREE

KATE

For the entire weekend Kate had done her utmost not to think about Theo. But even though she hadn't muttered his name, he'd entered her thoughts far too frequently. It had the feel of an unfinished project. An unended poem. A wish that had never been granted. She wanted to let it go, but at the same time found herself unable to.

'I'm going to call him,' Kate said on the evening of their return.

'Are you sure that's a good idea?' Freya asked nervously, while busy making them both a cup of tea. Tomorrow they'd both be on an early shift, Kate's first official shift as a full-time member of staff.

'I don't know, but I feel like I need to do *something*, even if it's just to offer to be his friend.'

'Is it possible to be friends with an ex? Especially one that's hurt you so badly.'

Kate shrugged her shoulders and accepted the mug of tea Freya passed over. 'I just can't help but feel there's more to it.'

'But what if that something is only going to hurt you more?

What if he's been shagging another bird and he just didn't want to tell you?'

Kate had asked about that as a possibility and he'd denied anything like that. He'd looked too broken, but perhaps his conscience had been eating him up. 'I just figured if I ring him, I can just ask.'

'Go on then, I want to hear this and it had better be good.'

She'd meant she'd call him later while by herself, but what difference would having Freya here make? She could always take the call elsewhere if it came to it.

Kate's heart started beating so hard she felt it in the apex of her chest, as if she'd gone on a sprint with no warm-up. Her palms sweated from pores she didn't know had those capabilities. She grabbed her phone before her hands were too slippery and placed it on the table ready to take the call on speakerphone mode.

It only took a few presses in the right place and her phone was ringing Theo.

With each ring, she tried to think of what to say. That she knew it was over, but was there any chance they could be friends would sum it up well enough. Although would she be able to be friends with a man who she didn't think was being truthful with her?

Ring. Ring. The phone kept going with no answer.

Kate and Freya looked at each other.

'Surely he's going to answer,' Freya said to the phone as much as she said it to Kate.

'I hoped he would.'

There were two more rings before the call cut off.

'So much for being *friends*.' Kate had been certain he'd do her the courtesy of answering a phone call.

'Well, balls to him. Delete his number out of your phone now.'

Kate hesitated for a minute. She wasn't going to ring him again if he was going completely incommunicado. But storing his number felt like keeping a memento. She shook her head and realised she was being silly. She needed to remember how he'd left her at the station. She found the option to delete and pressed it.

'I'm glad I wasn't trying to get in touch with him for anything important.'

'You are important. You were getting in touch so you could close the door on everything that's happened. Now we know that he's not even going to take your call, we need to seal that door shut ourselves. Men can be such players with our hearts. You wouldn't believe the amount of times I've heard things like this happen. Being the perfect boyfriend then ghosting for no good reason. I think we should go out tomorrow and celebrate your first official shift being completed. It'll give us a chance to search for some better options.'

Kate nodded some kind of agreement, although she didn't plan on picking up a random person to make herself feel better.

She needed longer to get over the ghost of the man who was still haunting her dreams.

CHAPTER FORTY-FOUR

THEO

If leaving her at the train station hadn't been bad enough, ignoring her call felt like the most heartless thing he'd ever done and that didn't sit right with Theo. But he wanted to save her what he was going through and having made that decision he was determined to stick with it.

He'd been due a phone upgrade so if she called again, it wouldn't hurt to go and get a new number at the same time if necessary. A clean break. One where they both got on with their lives. And he really wanted that for Kate. For her to go and find her happy with someone who could give her that.

Because right now, Theo wasn't happy. He was at one of his favourite places – soft play with George – but he wasn't running after him like he usually would.

Instead, he remained at the uncomfortable picnic benches with the other worn-out parents. He was certain the play centre had chosen the seating so that no parent or guardian remained there for too long. He'd contemplated going in, but his thoughts had flashed back to when he'd come crashing down the stairs. Nothing that disastrous had happened since, but he was remaining cautious. He didn't want to get trapped in a soft play and have to be rescued.

He was trying to enjoy being here and spending time with his nephew. It was something he'd missed over the past few weeks when he hadn't made their weekend session as regularly as usual. First, it had been because he'd been spending time with Kate and more recently, it had been because of all the medical appointments and the resulting changes he was making in his life.

With each of those things, the balls were in motion. The flat was on the market. The planning permission had been submitted. He was attending regular appointments and the MND Association had been in touch and made an appointment for one of their advisors to come and see Theo. Everything was as it should be, only, of course, it wasn't.

But after the phone call, he couldn't help but contemplate how he'd hoped that Kate would meet George. It was easy to imagine the two of them here and for everything he was mourning, the loss of potential was the worst. He tried not to think of the promise he'd made to Matthew and had been unable to entirely keep. Because if Kate was hurting anywhere as much as he was, he hadn't avoided breaking her heart. He was just making sure it wasn't any worse. What she didn't know couldn't hurt her.

'Come and have a slide race!' George ran to the table and begged.

'But you know you'll win!' Theo replied, pushing unfulfilled dreams aside.

'You won't fall. I'll help you up and then you slide down. That's not falling.'

Theo felt a lump in his throat. A ball of concern that was so big that he was sure it was visible. He didn't want to tell George that his biggest concern was getting up off the floor again. What if that was the moment his limbs wouldn't cooperate?

He knew that Anita had told George about his weak knee and how it had caused him to fall and that, because of it, Theo was having to be careful. He didn't know the rest. He didn't know that this was only the start.

Theo wished he didn't know those things either. Would he be quite so concerned if he didn't?

It might have been foolish, but for a while, Theo decided to switch that knowledge off. If he was going to live his life differently because of knowing, he was prepared to give himself temporary amnesia and hope for the best. Living for the moment seemed·more important than it ever had.

'Okay, I'll do it, but if Uncle Theo needs a hand, can I ask that you be the one to help?'

Perhaps it was too much to ask of a seven-year-old, but he knew George would be able to provide a steadying hand and he hoped upon hope that it was all he'd be in need of.

Ascending the stairs wasn't difficult. It hadn't been at any stage, it was going down them that was the problem. George took his hand and gently guided him. Getting onto his bum at the top of the slide was more of a challenge. Previously it had been something he'd done without thought, but he moved cautiously, holding onto the plastic side. Once he'd landed, he vowed to enjoy this next bit.

'Can we make this one not a race?' George asked. 'Can I hold your hand instead?'

The lump had returned. Theo did his best to swallow it down. 'Of course. Hopefully I keep up with you!'

Holding hands, they slid down and despite the height difference they managed to keep their palms connected. It was a moment Theo wanted to remain in forever. The rush. The laughter. The grip. They were all things he didn't want to let go of.

But at the bottom he faced getting himself up off the floor.

He was surprised to find it wasn't as difficult as he thought it might be.

George patiently waited by his side, offering a hand that Theo didn't end up needing.

'Can we go again?' George asked, the hope in his eyes showing.

Theo gave a nod with more certainty than he'd ever felt. Life was putting him through a lot, but that didn't mean he didn't get to live alongside that. It didn't mean joy was cancelled. It didn't mean he shouldn't embrace opportunities like he never had before.

This time they went up the stairs a little faster and every time they slid down hand in hand, joyous laughter escaped them both. They did it again and again until they were both worn out and in need of a drink.

And in that play session Theo learned that for whatever time he had left, he needed to let the joy win. But whatever joy he found, he knew he didn't want Kate to have to deal with what was to come. At least, that's what was convincing him to not return the phone call. To stay no contact. The knowledge that her way of finding joy was only ever going to be without him.

CHAPTER FORTY-FIVE

KATE

'Let's get Jägers!' Freya shouted across the music.

'Let's *not!*' Kate yelled back.

It was all very well celebrating her first shift as a full-time member of staff, but she had another one tomorrow morning. Freya did not, hence why her willingness to celebrate was at a different level of inebriation than Kate's. 'I'll have some lemonade and then I'm going home for some sleep.'

'Party pooper!'

'You know I have a shift tomorrow!'

'Ah, details... I'll get you a lemonade instead, then.'

Thankfully Freya did and she also scaled her drink down to a gin and tonic.

'Can we get a taxi after this? I need some beauty sleep before my early start.'

'If we have to. It wasn't a very successful fishing expedition.'

'We were celebrating and I never planned to do anything other than that.'

'Spoilsport.'

'I prefer level-headed woman.'

They finished the last of their drinks and got themselves a

taxi back home. The driver obviously knew his way around the quickest routes and took a few deviations through some of the backstreets. Even though it was the outskirts of London, Littleton-on-Thames had its fair share of cobbled streets and quaint corners that it could be mistaken for a Cotswold hamlet. Although the fact it was dark made that illusion easier to believe.

The taxi passed Theo's block of flats and Kate wasn't able to stop herself from having a look. Freya didn't know it was his property she was glancing at so she wasn't going to tell her off for looking at the door they'd vowed she would close.

Out at the front of the small courtyard there was a FOR SALE sign. On the side it had the number of the flat that was for sale. It was too dark to make out the handwritten numeral, but Kate felt sure it was going to be Theo's.

Once they'd returned, she didn't sleep well for thinking about it. Why would he sell his flat? The place where he'd seemed happy. Of course, it might be another of the properties and she might be jumping the gun, but it would match the sudden change in him.

Between not sleeping and powering through a shift with sleep deprivation going through her veins, she decided the only sensible thing was to go there and see for herself.

Rather than getting the bus towards her home, she got the bus towards Theo's flat in the hope it would give her a definite answer. It was a touch too much on the side of stalking for Kate, but she figured if it was a one-off thing, then it was okay. He'd decided to disappear from her life and she wanted to have some idea of why.

She took the walk slowly, almost hoping to bump into Theo or to spot his car. Not that that happening would necessarily give her answers. Not if he ignored her which, judging by her phone call that had never been returned, was quite possible.

When she arrived at the block of flats, it didn't take long to confirm what she'd guessed. It was his flat up for sale. It just begged the question why? If he'd been planning on travelling or moving elsewhere, surely he'd have said something? She realised he didn't owe her an explanation, but she'd never have thought he'd have kept anything like that from her.

It might be taking it a step too far, but Kate decided to ring his doorbell. The questions kept blooming in her head. One produced another and then another. There were so many now it was overcrowded with them.

The doorbell went unanswered.

Kate glanced up towards the flat to see if there were any signs of life, but the visible blinds were closed and there were nothing else to see up there.

She just hoped nothing had happened to him. She thought about the version of Theo she'd seen at the train station when he'd called things off. He'd been wearing saggy grey jogging bottoms and a matching hoodie. He'd been entirely different to the smart Rupert the Bear inspired gentleman she'd met when she'd been a crying mess wondering how she was going to get home. The one in his checked trousers with his crisp linen shirt and with amber tones in his aftershave. The difference between those two days were such a contrast it was hard to fathom. The idea that potentially he'd been having some kind of mental health crisis crossed her mind. What if he had and she'd just walked away?

That wasn't what had happened, she reminded herself. He'd had the option to come with her, but hadn't. Instead, he'd called it off.

Even though it went against her policy of only trying things once, Kate pressed the doorbell again, holding it down so if he was in, there would be no doubt he'd hear.

Again, there was no response. No answers to her questions.

She walked away, but continued glancing back towards the windows that she knew belonged to Theo's flat. She wasn't sure what she was hoping to see. A twitch of a curtain. A glimpse of the man himself, but none of those things happened and she'd run out of options. She'd done all she could to get in touch with him. To see if there was any chance of a post break-up conversation that would give her a clearer picture of what went wrong.

She'd rung. She'd gone to his flat. It didn't feel like there were any options left. He'd truly ghosted her and she had no idea what to do to summon him. It was clear that wasn't what he wanted so it was best to walk away with her head still held high.

But even though that was what she wanted to do, there was another part of her, most likely her gut, telling her to try one last thing. As what she'd done so far hadn't worked, she needed to try something new.

She was only a few roads away from the flat and as she passed a post office, the idea struck her. She'd do it in the form of a letter. She liked the idea of doing something that went beyond the effort of a simple text message. She went into the shop and purchased a pen, a notepad and some envelopes.

Once she had them, she went and found the nearest bus stop so she had a place to sit and something to lean on. It took a few attempts, but it resulted in a letter she was happy with.

We met on Platform 1 in Southfern in July.

We said goodbye near Platform 3 in Littleton-on-Thames in September.

So much happened in between. And I never really said that part of that time involved falling in love.

I don't know what happened, but if there's a chance that you love me too, please get in touch.

It was a simple message and Kate deliberately didn't add

any kind of names or clarifying details. Before wandering back to his flat, she took a picture of the letter. It felt as if his flat had been abandoned and he wasn't living there anymore. His car wasn't there and there were no other signs of life other than the newly added FOR SALE sign. She didn't want to risk the letter never getting any further than the other side of his door. So while the physical letter was being posted through his door, the picture was going to enable her to post it elsewhere. After sliding it through the letterbox for his flat, Kate set about the second part of the plan. Not that any letterboxes were required for that.

She posted it on Facebook, X, Instagram, TikTok and every other social media platform she knew of. She didn't elaborate any further, just added the picture of the letter and hoped that somehow Theo would see it.

Within twenty-three minutes it had gone viral. Before she'd even managed to get home, thousands of people had seen the note.

She just had to hope that number included the one person she wished it would reach.

CHAPTER FORTY-SIX

THEO

Theo's sister didn't often get angry, but when she did there was no denying it. There was also no avoiding it.

Anita had the look of a crow when it happened. Dark and swooping, difficult to swerve. The last time it had happened was when he'd fed George popcorn at a time he was still in nappies and apparently the two didn't create a happy marriage. Especially for the person left to change the nappy.

That had obviously been some time ago and because it was, he was ill-equipped to know how to deal with whatever was incoming. But her course of direction meant he knew it was him. He was the cause of her anger, and he wasn't going to be able to hide even if he took shelter under the table. He really did want to take shelter under the table.

'*Why* haven't you said anything?' Anita arrived in their grandparents' kitchen before he had the chance to hide.

'About what?' He went through his index of what he might have done to upset his sister. Perhaps George had let on that he'd been on the soft play equipment after she'd strictly forbidden it. Perhaps he'd forgotten to tell her the flat was on the market. Everything had been happening at such a pace that it had been hard to keep up with who he'd informed and who he hadn't.

'To *Kate*! *Please* tell me you told her.'

If Anita was a crow, then Theo was a dormouse. He just needed to find somewhere to burrow and hide.

'I've already told you... it's over.'

'Because *you* finished it. Without *telling* her *why!*'

Theo took a step back, making sure it was in the direction of the nearest exit.

'How do you know this anyway?' he asked, deflecting from telling the truth.

'Have you been honest and told Kate or not?'

'No, because... it seemed *too* cruel. She hasn't recovered from the death of her brother yet. She doesn't want to be wrapped up in all this.' Theo flapped his hand about as if the static air surrounding him was to blame.

'But you didn't give her the choice. You didn't tell her so she could make up her own mind, then you *abandoned* her at a train station!'

'How do you know that? Have you been speaking to her?'

'Don't go avoiding my questions by firing your own at me. Tell me what happened, then I'll tell you how I know.'

Theo took a step back closer to the doorway. He never had altercations with his sister, but he was prepared to run if necessary. Although he wasn't sure where that would get him other than in more trouble.

'I didn't want her to stay with me out of sympathy. I didn't want to put her through that not after what I promised her brother.'

'What did you promise her brother? I thought you only met him once.'

'I did and he asked two things of me. He asked that I hang around to explore whatever potential there was between Kate and I.'

'And what else?'

'He made me promise to never hurt her in the way his death would.'

'Shit.' Anita deflated from an angry crow into a crumpled pigeon, flumping onto a breakfast bar stool as she said it.

'Exactly. Because that's what this will do. It's a guaranteed path to heartbreak and I couldn't do that to her, not after she's been through so much already.'

Anita didn't respond. She dragged a weary hand through her hair and placed what she'd been holding onto the counter.

'What's that?' Theo hadn't noticed the newspaper until now. He'd been too concerned by his sister's expression.

'It's the reason I know.'

'How can you know from the paper?' Theo felt himself go pale, his blood draining away so his heart could beat faster.

'Page thirty-two,' Anita replied without looking up.

Theo flicked through to find the page she meant. When he reached it the only picture was a note. The headline stating a local love note had gone viral.

It took a moment for Theo's eyesight to focus. By the time he'd finished reading it, he felt winded. Of course he loved her. But even if he was opting to find joy in life, it didn't mean he should rob someone of theirs.

'Do you love her?'

Theo nodded, knowing he wouldn't be able to keep that from his sister.

'Then you have to tell her.'

'I just don't want to hurt her. I wanted to keep my promise.'

'I think she's hurting already. And when you spoke to her brother, neither of you knew what was going to happen. How the future was going to unfold. I think you need to tell her at the very least. Then she can decide what she wants to do.'

Theo plonked himself on the stool next to his sister and rested his head in his hands. The burden was heavy because he knew even after telling Kate, she might choose to walk away. He wasn't sure what he'd do if the situation was reversed. He liked to think he'd stick by her, but at the same time they'd only known each other for five minutes in the grand scheme of things.

'So, what are you going to do?'

'Other than be sick?' His stomach was really turning at the thought of telling Kate. It had been bad enough telling the whole family and that had been with Owen as his spokesperson. He wasn't about to enlist him for this.

'No jokes. What are you going to do?' Anita persisted.

'I'm going to tell her. I just need to work out how.'

'Just state it plain and simple like you did when you told us.'

Theo nodded without taking his head out of his hands. He knew what he needed to do, but that didn't make it any easier.

CHAPTER FORTY-SEVEN

KATE

Over the past two days, Kate's social media posts had blown up like she'd never imagined they would. She'd had to switch off comments as they'd got to a point where some were ludicrous and insulting. She'd lost count of the number of weird internet troll-like personalities that had offered to show her a good time. She'd nearly puked on reading a couple.

None of that mattered now, though. She'd take the strange responses one hundred times over because it had elicited the one that she'd been after. At last, she'd heard from Theo!

It had been a simple text message inviting her over to his flat that evening.

Meet me at my flat at 7:30 tonight. See you then if you can make it.

There was no indication as to how he was feeling in those words. And Kate didn't know how to feel either when she was a mix of emotions. Elated that he'd been in touch and wanted to meet. Terrified that he'd just be furious about the note going so viral. The message certainly wasn't full of enthusiasm, but it was an invitation that she was going to take up so she'd be able to add a full stop to what had happened between them. Or rather what hadn't.

Because she didn't know what she was going to be walking into, it was also impossible to know what to wear and she stared at her open wardrobe for another long minute. It reminded her of when she packed for their first weekend away. She'd not known what to take, but there had never been the sense of dread that she'd been left with now.

In the end, she opted for jeans and a T-shirt. It wasn't exactly glamorous, but it didn't feel like it was that kind of occasion.

She opted to walk to his flat. It was a two-mile trek, but she felt as if she needed to get any fear out of her system. She'd said on the note to get in touch if he felt the same way so surely there was some hope he did. But she didn't sense that in the way she'd like to.

Niggling doubt settled itself into her walking rhythm. The sense of something being wrong hadn't left her, nor had the want to hear an explanation. Maybe Freya had been right... maybe he had met someone else. Maybe she'd arrive and the police would be there ready to tell her to stop harassing him, especially on a scale that meant thousands of people knew about their romance: both the beginning and the end taking place at train stations. Along with the multitude of strange men offering to take her on a date, she'd also had message after message of sympathy. Women who'd also been ghosted, the reasons why never expanded on. They'd all wished her luck and told her not to get her hopes up.

And here she was riding high on hope, while trying to keep her expectations in check. It was nausea inducing and by the time she reached Theo's street, she was almost certain she was going to be sick.

She stopped by the bus stop shelter, hoping he wasn't

looking for her out the window. If he was, she shouldn't be visible from here and she needed to take a few minutes to get her breath back. Her pace had been close to a run in her eagerness to get here and now she was, it felt too soon and not soon enough. Every feeling had a complete contradiction running alongside it.

She watched her heart rate on her fitness watch and gradually it began to lower. Not quite resting heart rate, but not so high it was comparable to running a fever. That was when she noticed she was late. Not terribly. Only by a few minutes and in a way she was glad. She didn't want to come across as so desperate that she was there on the dot. Although the fact that she'd posted the letter on social media, and it had ended up in the local newspaper might have desperation written all over it.

Taking a final calming breath, she made her way over the road and to the flat's call buzzer. She pressed it without hesitation, eager to get on with it now that she was finally here. As she waited for a response, she stared at the FOR SALE sign. It was the reason she'd written the letter in the first place. She had questions before seeing it, but it had unlocked so many more.

But, of course, the questions weren't the reason she was here. The reason she was here were the memories they'd created in the short time they'd been together. Those had been real. Those were the moments that had brought her here. She knew they'd meant something and she needed to understand why he was walking away from her.

The speaker buzzed to life and a noise sounded. 'Come in. See you in a minute.'

The door handle felt as cold as the reception. She wasn't sure what she'd been hoping for, but now she was able to get into the building, the temptation to flee flared up. She'd already had her heart broken by Theo... was she just giving him another opportunity to do it again?

The door to his flat was slightly ajar when she reached it so she pushed it open tentatively. 'Hello?' she said, before it was fully open.

'Hi.' Theo was sitting at the breakfast bar facing her. 'I made you a tea. I figured that's what you would want.'

'Um, thanks.' Kate pushed the door closed and placed her bag on the floor. She had that awkward sense of arriving for an interview that she hadn't prepared adequately for.

Despite having been to Theo's flat several times before, even that felt unfamiliar. Some of the furniture was no longer here and any personal touches – his house plants, any wall hangings, his books – had disappeared.

'How have you been?' he asked, when she landed in the space opposite him.

Kate adjusted herself in the seat, no longer feeling like she was welcome in this flat. This was a formality, she realised.

'I'm as well as can be.' It was a generic answer because if he'd asked where she'd place her position on a scale, she wasn't sure where she'd put herself. Good things had happened, despite everything. But because of all that was going on, she'd not perhaps enjoyed those triumphs in the same way. 'I've started my full-time hours on D4 ward.'

'That's great news. How's it going?' Theo's expression edged into a smile that wasn't fully there in his eyes.

Kate had a sip of tea from the mug he'd made her. It was already lukewarm, making her wonder if it had been waiting since seven thirty, her lateness making it colder. This was weird. 'It's... great. To be honest, it doesn't feel very different from how it was before.' Unlike *us* she almost added, but held her tongue.

'It must be nice that it's more regular.'

The polite chit-chat was killing Kate. 'I think I'll be more on board with that when I've had a few more pay cheques.' She glanced around. 'So, is your flat for sale?'

Theo nodded gravely. It wasn't the response of someone about to travel the world.

'Where are you heading?' she asked when he didn't say anything to fill the blanks.

'I need to tell you something, Kate.'

From the tone of his voice, it didn't sound like he'd be announcing his undying love like she'd hoped. 'Okay,' she said, hoping the blanks would be filled this time.

'A lot has changed for me over the past few weeks.'

He paused and when he didn't say anything further, Kate attempted some coaxing. 'Like what?'

'The issues I'd been having with my knee, it turned out there was more to it.'

Another beat of silence, but this time Kate waited.

'Last month, before you asked me to come away with you, I was diagnosed with motor neurone disease.'

Kate gasped as her hand flew to her mouth. How could it be? 'They're certain?' she asked, barely able to speak for the shock of knowing what this meant.

Theo nodded and like a game of Tetris, everything began to slot into place.

Kate decided to screw the interview format and slid off her stool to go and hold Theo. At first he resisted. He was doing this as a formality, just as she'd suspected from the minute she'd arrived at his door. But it wasn't long before tears sprang from him and she ended up joining him. She wanted to say it would be okay, but she didn't want to supply false platitudes. It was life-changing and that's why so much of life had altered for him.

'Why didn't you tell me?'

Theo pulled his grey jumper to cover his palm and used that to wipe away the tears from his face.

'Two reasons. First, I didn't want you to feel under any obligation to stay. I know you well enough to know that you would. And secondly, when I met your brother, I made a promise to him. He made me promise that I'd never hurt you in the way his death would.'

Kate let that knowledge float over her, and it came down on her like hail. Cold and sharp and stinging. She hadn't understood what he'd meant when he'd mentioned promises before, but now it made total sense. 'And you knew this would break that promise?' It came out as a whisper.

'Yes. And I couldn't do that to you. I couldn't allow you to end up trapped.'

A rushing memory of every happy moment she'd shared with Theo came to her then. Talking to sheep in a field. Meeting his sister and hearing that she was a keeper. His support at her brother's funeral. They were all there waiting to remind her of why she'd wanted to check in with him one more time. Because she'd known in her heart that things hadn't just dwindled.

Kate cupped his face first to make sure it was what he wanted too. The look Theo gave told her everything she needed to know and so she kissed him. Gently to begin with. A familiarisation as their lips met for the first time in weeks. Last time it had been when he'd been covered in bruises and, in this moment, she realised that must have been part of what led him to the diagnosis he'd told her about now. It had been the beginning of the end of what they'd shared. Despite that, it didn't stop the kissing from continuing. The gentle moving towards more urgent.

'Wait.' It was Theo that stopped them. 'However nice kissing you again is, we need to talk about this.'

'You're right, I'm sorry.'

'Don't ever be sorry about kissing me,' he said, with a small smile.

'In that case, do you mind?' Kate kissed him again, more playfully this time, helping to make any tension leave the room.

'This is serious,' he said, laughing as he pulled her closer.

'It is. So let me make us both a decent cup of tea and then we can get on with the serious talk.'

As Kate set about making them hot drinks, despite the enormity of what Theo had told her, she knew they were going to be back on track. One way or another. No matter what. She knew she hadn't been wrong about the fact Theo was her forever. Because on the odd occasion, it was okay if promises were broken.

And she knew Matthew would forgive them if being together meant Theo broke his.

CHAPTER FORTY-EIGHT

THEO

The kiss was perfection and Theo was unable to resist pulling Kate closer, but he also realised he needed to give her the chance to walk away. He knew that what he'd told her would take more than a day to sink in. Its repercussions would fill every quarter of their relationship if they continued to have one.

'What happens after you've sold the flat?' Kate asked, nursing her mug of tea. They'd retired to the sofa now, so they were closer together, but they were being sensible over not having their hands all over each other as they spoke.

The desire to hold Kate was strong, but he didn't want to distract her. That had happened too easily as soon as they were back in each other's presence.

'We're putting in planning permission to build an annexe at my grandparents' property, so I can live there independently for now and assisted when the time comes.'

Kate stared at him for a while, as if she were doing a difficult mathematics assignment. 'Is that what you want? To go and live there?'

Theo almost laughed knowing that he'd left behind every-thing he wanted in Mr Welsh's consultation room. 'I think it's my best option. To be near family and have them looking out for me.'

'But what would you have wanted?'

Theo smiled a sad smile. Because what he wanted and what was possible were two different things now. 'I get what you mean, but I'm just being realistic about my options.'

'But what if there are other options? Ones you haven't considered?'

'What other options?'

'Ones that include... me?'

Theo hadn't considered that. He hadn't allowed himself to imagine a future that included Kate.

'I think you need to give yourself some time to think. It's a lot to take in and you shouldn't make any decisions without considering everything.'

'What if I don't need to?' Kate held his knee as she said it and he knew that she meant it.

'Can I ask that you do so, for me? I know that's a lot to ask considering I kept it from you, but I made plans thinking they were for the best. I don't want to change them only for you to change your mind. I don't think I'd cope with that very well.' He was being honest because in his life he'd never known what it had been like to be fragile and vulnerable until this past month. Now he could give lessons on what it was to feel like that.

'You're right. No snap decisions. But I need you to know, I want to be in your life. No matter what, I still want to be your friend, if nothing else.'

Theo knew he'd take Kate's friendship in a heartbeat. He hoped for more, of course, but he wasn't going to lay that on thick when what he'd told her was fresh and new. She might not want the same once she'd slept on it.

'I'll tell you what... why don't you meet me at the train station tomorrow at seven thirty?' Theo suggested.

'Is this a re-enactment?'

'Possibly. I just want you to know, it's okay if you don't show. It can be like plotting your revenge, if you like. Or, if you do decide to come, I want to make up for the fact I kept it to myself. I did that because I felt like I had a duty to you and your brother. But none of us could ever have predicted this as a turn of events and I should have realised you needed to know rather than being left in the dark.'

'Okay, but promise me this. If I do turn up, we go full throttle. We don't skirt around maybes. We go into this *together* and make decisions *together*.'

'Deal,' he said, offering his hand out to shake as if it were a formal business arrangement.

'I'll see you tomorrow then.'

'Don't go making any promises yet. You have to sleep on it... remember.'

'Okay, no promises, but please make sure you remember that you're not alone in this, whatever I decide.'

Their drinks had been replenished more than once and an agreement made. It had been over two hours since Kate had arrived and Theo realised he was calmer than he had been in weeks.

'Thank you. That means a lot. And I'm sorry for being a coward, or whatever trait it was that stopped me from telling you.'

'You don't need to say sorry. Many things, but never that.'

When she left the flat, Theo realised he now had a sense of optimism about his potential options for the first time since he had heard his devastating diagnosis.

He barely slept that night. The following morning, once it was early enough, he headed to the hospital. Not for an appointment for once. Instead, he was heading to D4 ward, the one where Kate worked. He was heading there in the hope of talking to one of her friends and, as luck would have it, as soon as he reached the ward he saw one of her housemates.

'What are you doing here?' she practically spat at him.

Theo wasn't surprised by the hostility.

'I wanted to ask you a question.'

'Surely you'd rather see Kate, seeing as you haven't been in touch with her!'

'It's Freya, isn't it?' Theo was glad he'd remembered her name. 'Do you know where Kate booked when she planned a weekend away for us?'

Freya glanced around the ward, making sure she wasn't needed elsewhere no doubt. 'Why are you asking me this?'

Theo was stumped for a second. He wasn't sure what he'd imagined when he'd made his way here. Of course Kate's friends weren't going to welcome him with open arms and help him. Not when they didn't know. And he wasn't sure he was ready to reveal all with Kate still processing it.

'You're Kate's best friend, right?'

'One of them.'

'Can I tell you something in complete confidence?'

'We're in a hospital corridor. The walls likely have ears. Wait here a minute.'

Theo did as asked. He was glad to note that Freya's animosity at him being there seemed to have settled.

After going further into the ward, Freya returned and waved him over to a door behind the reception desk.

'Come into the staffroom. I'm taking my break early so you can tell me while I eat my lunch.'

Theo followed Freya into a small common room that housed some lockers, basic seating and a microwave on top of a fridge.

'At least you'll be able to talk here without the patients overhearing.'

'Thanks. It's appreciated.'

Freya went to her locker and grabbed whatever she had for lunch, loading it into the microwave to warm up for three minutes. 'What is it you wanted to ask or say then?'

Theo realised her time was limited and he didn't want to waste it. 'Directly before the weekend that Kate had planned for us to go away, I was diagnosed with motor neurone disease. Rightly or wrongly, I didn't want to involve Kate. She's already been through so much with her brother, I didn't want her to have to face the same with me. I thought a clean break would be for the best. She could continue her life without that burden.'

'She knew something was going on. You saw the viral note, right?'

'Yes, and I have the real thing that she posted to my flat. So, I've told her. My sister suggested I shouldn't leave things how I did and I knew she was right. But I didn't want Kate to make any hasty decisions. Because whatever we thought our future might hold has gone and I want her to walk into this with her eyes open. I said she needed to take at least twenty-four hours to think about it and the plan is that we're meeting at the train station tonight. Whatever she decides, I'm glad I've told her so we can be friends at the very least.' Theo realised he was beginning to witter on, already making sure he didn't hope for anything more.

'I'm glad you've told her. It was the right thing to do. But I don't understand why you're here telling me now. What question was it you needed to ask?'

Theo shook his head. He'd not worked out the short format of telling people what was going on with him. The buffers he added felt like a requirement.

'I wanted to know where she booked on the weekend we were supposed to go away together. I was hoping to rebook it, in the hope we'll be able to have a redo. Although I'm not sure redo is the word I'm after, but hopefully you know what I mean.'

'Yes, I know the place. I have the details on my phone.' Freya abandoned her microwave meal to grab her phone out of her locker.

She showed him the details and he took a quick picture of them so he had them saved and wouldn't have to bother her again.

'And I know you will be, but I wanted to ask that you'll be there for her, no matter what she decides.'

Freya issued the reassurances he'd hoped to hear and, as the blue skies met him outside, he prayed for sunny days ahead. Ones that contained joy.

CHAPTER FORTY-NINE

KATE

After a night of digesting Theo's news, Kate went to visit the person she wished she could speak to.

She wrapped up warm in her coat and jumper and took a slab of Dairy Milk chocolate – Matthew's favourite – to enjoy while at his graveside. She didn't see the point of taking flowers when he hadn't ever liked them when he'd been alive. Eating enough chocolate for two while there seemed to be the best way to honour him.

His ashes had been buried in a much smaller ceremony and the headstone was now in place. Kate brushed her fingers over his name as if that would connect them somehow.

'Can I ask how it is that you're still managing to interfere with my love life?' There were no other mourners nearby so Kate continued, trying to ignore the disappointment with regard to it being a one-way conversation. None of her brother's usual witty retorts.

'Apparently you told Theo to never hurt me in the way losing you would. Because of that, he dumped me, and you'll never believe why?'

Kate paused to unwrap one end of the chocolate and took a

massive bite. If he wasn't able to respond she was going to imagine what he would say while stuffing her face with chocolate.

'It's because he's ill. His time with me is going to be short, the same as yours was. He said he didn't want to put me through that again.'

Another substantial bite was necessary, but chewing the chocolate didn't stop the tears that started to fall.

'And do you know what? I'd do it again with you. It might have been hard, but I'd do anything to have you back.' Kate used the sleeve of her coat to brush away at her cheeks. 'Theo's given me a day to make up my mind, but I don't need a day.'

Another chunk of Dairy Milk was destroyed.

'I already know that it's much better to love completely. You taught me that. And I think, even though you're not here for me to be certain, that you'd want me to be happy even if that means walking the same path we had to.'

Kate set about savaging more of the chocolate. She was rather glad there was no one about to watch this act of comfort eating. But it seemed only right that she ate her brother's share on his behalf.

'So, I hope you don't mind, but I'm going to be concentrating on falling in love for a while. The worst movie type of love story that you used to hate. The type where there's an improbable happy-ever-after. The ones where they fall in love against the odds. The kind of love that's happening to me is the kind of movie that you'd walk out of, or tell me to switch over. And sadly, the odds really are against us, but not in the way I thought they would be. But that's okay. Sometimes news like this gives us an opportunity to know we have to appreciate what we have while we can. I'm not going to be sad about our reality. Because right now, we're two people in love. At least, I think we are. I'm pretty certain that from seven thirty tonight that will be true.'

It was surprising the speed at which the bar of chocolate had disappeared. It was so quick, Kate wondered if she'd pulled off a magic trick and no one had been about to witness it. But in a strange way, she didn't think that was true. Her brother might not be about physically anymore, but she felt his presence in her life. Not like a ghost or ghoul or anything she might be frightened of. It was more of an invisible hand of reassurance. One that was giving its blessing, both on her plans to be by Theo's side, as well as her ability to eat a whole bar of chocolate solo and in record timing.

'I love you, Matthew. Promise me you'll look after us,' Kate said, before kissing the cold stone and heading off to go and fall in love. Completely. With zero regret.

CHAPTER FIFTY

THEO

The cold night air was making Theo shiver. The temperatures had dropped recently as the year rolled towards autumn. But he knew that wasn't the only thing making him shake, it was waiting for Kate that was doing it.

In the time since he'd seen her at his flat yesterday, every possibility had gone through his head. There was no guarantee she'd show and even if she did, Kate might choose to treat him in the same way he had her the last time they'd been here. She might opt to tell him face to face that she didn't want to come with him. That he'd been right in his presumption that she'd feel trapped and she couldn't face it.

Theo started pacing to try and ignore the scenarios he was imagining. He needed to focus on the here and now. The announcements with the electronic voices letting everyone know what trains would be arriving where. The whoosh of an arriving train and the tiny stampedes of passengers getting on and off. The coffee machine in the small platform café that seemed to be the hardest working employee in the station. All the everyday noises and the sound of his footsteps weren't enough to distract from the fear that she wouldn't show.

And he had to be okay with that. He knew his friends and family would be there for him. They had a plan. One that he was as happy as he could be about. But he had to admit that he'd opened the door to the hope of something better.

His watch told him a different story, though. Because it was no longer seven thirty. It was four minutes and twenty-two seconds past that time.

It took his knee giving slightly for him to stop his march back and forth. He just needed to be patient.

'Can Theo Parrish please come to the ticket desk?' the tinny speaker called out.

Theo had been so busy concentrating on the people coming in and out of the station, he hadn't been listening to the announcements. He'd zoned out of them fearing Kate's non-arrival. Now he was wondering how many times his name had been called without him noticing.

What did they want him for? Kate was the only person who knew he was here and why. Had she called them and left a message? Maybe that was how this goodbye was going to go.

Slowly, Theo made his way towards the doors leading to the ticket desk. The pit of his stomach became lead destined only for his boots when he didn't spot her. Only a group of people nowhere near the ticket booth.

'Hi,' Theo said hesitantly to the lady behind the counter. 'My name was just called out over the Tannoy. It said to come here.'

The woman's expression didn't change as if he was in another country and had neglected to switch language.

Instead of saying anything, the woman nodded towards the group of people, offering only a half-smile in response.

Theo glanced round and it took him a second to spot Kate. Because the first person he spotted was Owen. Then Sharon. Followed by Anita and George.

Kate was in the middle.

'What's going on?' Theo asked, before heading over.

For a second, he wasn't sure if his legs would carry him over. Not because of anything to do with the condition he now knew he had, but because of the shock of seeing everyone here at the same time.

'We're going on *holiday*!' Kate declared.

'Who is?' Theo had thought of a lot of scenarios, but his friends and family turning up as well had not been one of them.

'All of us!' Owen replied. 'Sorry to bust your romantic weekend, but when Kate suggested it, we had to say yes.'

It was only when Owen had spoken that Theo took in the fact their receptionist was there with her arm linked with Owen's. As he clocked it, Owen continued to help with some of the blanks.

'We're going to the glamping place you and Kate first went to. A couple in each pod. And, yes, I've finally asked Sharon out after your years of pestering!'

'Me and Mum are *not* a couple!' George added, indignantly.

'Of course not. I just meant we were in pairs.'

'Can't I stay with Uncle Theo?'

'Not this time.' Anita rubbed her son's head. 'But we'll arrange a sleepover soon.'

'What about the B&B? It's booked for the weekend.'

'Don't worry.' Kate stepped forward, taking his hands into hers. 'Freya told me your plan and whilst it was a very good plan, I thought this might be a better one. It was Owen that helped with the booking.'

'So, you've all conspired against me?'

'This is definitely not conspiring,' Anita said.

'You're right. This definitely isn't.' Theo kissed Kate in the way he imagined a church kiss would go after a wedding. It would have been more passionate, but they had to bear in mind that they had an audience.

'Eww!' George added his sound effect.

'The car I've hired is ready when you are,' Owen said.

'We'll go and take a seat. It'll give these love birds a moment without George's soundtrack,' Anita said.

'How come we're going in a car?'

'That was Owen's idea,' Kate said as they watched the four of them filter out towards the car park.

'I feel bad being in a train station and about to head off in a car.'

'Don't worry. Train stations don't have feelings and we're sharing it so it's almost like taking public transport.'

They were skirting around the big questions. The ones that had brought them here. 'Are you sure?' Theo asked, guessing she'd know what he meant.

'I've never been surer. Full throttle, remember? Let's do the full journey together and see where life takes us.'

They held each other then. The passionate kisses could wait for later when they were truly alone. Right now, holding onto whatever future they had together was what they both wanted.

CHAPTER FIFTY-ONE

KATE

They were in the same pod they'd been in last time they were here. George had already knocked on the door wanting to compare their pod to his and had gone round declaring everything as 'cool', even though both pods were very similar – Theo knew, having designed them. Every aspect had been examined until Anita came to retrieve him.

'Sorry, he's very excited and avoiding bedtime!'

'It's okay. Holidays are exciting. But make sure you get your sleep. We've got lots of exploring to do tomorrow,' Theo said.

George gave them both a quick hug before heading off with his mum.

'Next stop PJs and hot chocolate,' they heard Anita say before closing their door.

'Alone at last,' Theo said as he joined Kate on the sofa.

'We hope,' Kate said, curling into Theo. 'PJs and hot chocolate sounds like an excellent idea.'

'The very best of ideas.'

'I'll put the kettle on.'

'Not yet. We can sort that in a minute. I wanted to say thank you first.'

'For what?'

'For organising this. I thought the best possible scenario I could hope for was you being at the station and wanting to make a go of this, despite what we both now know. I never thought you'd manage to get my friends and family involved as well. If it was just you and I, this weekend would have been special, but you've somehow managed to top that.'

'You gave me twenty-four hours you see. That's a lot of time to make plans when I already knew what my answer was going to be. So, it got me thinking... what would be the perfect weekend? And I know you had put plans in place, but that B&B doesn't hold happy memories for me. And I thought it was important to come somewhere with good memories. I hope that's okay?'

'Of course it is. And thank you for getting some of the people who are dear to me involved.'

'They were very willing volunteers. And even though I've only met George today, I'm a bit in love already.'

'Make sure you reserve some of that for me.'

'Okay, I love you too.'

'That's better. I love you too.'

They kissed then the way they would have done earlier if it hadn't been for their audience. It was deep and passionate and made up for all the lost days.

There were a lot of things to talk about and discuss, but they would wait. Because from this point forward they were going to be finding joy in the small moments. Those were the ones that mattered from now on.

EPILOGUE

The annexe was never built in Theo's grandparents' garden. Instead, Theo and Kate went travelling around Europe for a month: Italy, Spain and Holland. They ate authentic pizzas, went on vineyard tours and enjoyed a legal spliff.

When they were home, it was to their new place. A bungalow not far from Anita and George's house. Owen had handled each stage of the process, buying out Theo's share of the company to help provide a large deposit.

Theo stopped working, mostly. OT Architects remained the name of the company, but it was reduced to O plus T on the odd occasion when the project called for it.

Between Christmas and New Year, they went to Owen and Sharon's wedding with Theo as best man. Apparently after years of being in love and not telling each other, they'd decided there was no time like the present.

A week later, Theo realised they were right and got down on one knee and asked Kate to marry him. Living together wasn't enough, and he wasn't sure why he hadn't done it sooner, but seeing the romance he thought would never happen turn into an actual thing made it clear he should follow their lead.

Theo and Kate got married less than two months later. Not wanting to waste time on the planning, they went to Gretna Green on Valentine's Day and had the day they'd always wanted.

Kate continued working full-time on D4 ward and, whenever she had more than one day off in a row, they went somewhere, either in the camper van they'd purchased – called Betty – or the cheapest deal they could find for a city weekend break.

They watched sunrises and sunsets and full moons and shooting stars and they did their best to enjoy all the small moments, even when Theo's body was showing signs of its gentle decline. That was something they worked with.

By the following summer, Kate missed a period and, even though it wasn't something they'd planned, Theo got to hold his son in his arms. They called him Matt, a shortened version of Matthew that Kate's brother had never used, but a name she'd always associate with him.

George visited them every weekend and took on the role of big brother, easing rather than adding to the childcare.

And when standing and holding their son became more of an impossible task for Theo, Kate extended her maternity leave to care for her husband as well as her son.

And they continued enjoying all the small moments, making them count whatever they were.

Dates in the garden.

Taking the camper van to the beach for a sleepover.

Watching a plane fly through the night sky almost like a shooting star.

Kate planning surprise weekends away.

Theo organising romantic meals delivered to their door.

A picnic at home.

The wind in their hair.

A red admiral passing them by.

Unexpected laughter.

Baby Matt's first steps.

Perhaps it was knowing that they had a full stop made them make sure that it all counted. Like a song that never missed a beat. One that was guaranteed to provide them with the perfect end credits.

All those small quiet moments became pins in a map. They marked a shared lifetime. They were the memories that would matter. They were the things that would last.

A LETTER FROM CATHERINE

Dear Reader,

Thank you for reading Kate and Theo's story. Writing about two people falling in love, despite their circumstances, was a delight to write as life can so often be like that.

I wrote this in the quickest time frame I have for a while because of having to complete a civic duty and I'm thankful for all the people I met during that process and for Bookouture's support in making sure I got this completed as well.

If you did enjoy *The Day He Disappeared*, and want to keep up to date with all my latest releases, just sign up at the following link. Your email address will never be shared and you can unsubscribe at any time.

www.bookouture.com/catherine-miller

I hope you loved *The Day He Disappeared* and if you did I would be very grateful if you could write a review. Every one of them is appreciated and I'd love to hear what you think, and it makes such a difference helping new readers to discover one of my books for the first time.

I love hearing from my readers – you can get in touch through my social media, or my website.

Go and bathe in the small moments for me. Sometimes they slide away from us all too quickly.

Love, laughter, and light,

Catherine x

www.katylittlelady.com

facebook.com/katylittlelady.author
x.com/katylittlelady
instagram.com/katylittlelady

ACKNOWLEDGEMENTS

First and foremost, I'd like to thank my editor, Jess Whitlum-Cooper, and my agents, Hattie Grünewald and Rhian Parry. They've been there from the start of this story helping to shape it into what it's become. I'd also like to thank my copy editor, Jane Eastgate, and proof reader, Becca Allen, and the rest of the Bookouture team with a special mention to Kim, Jess, Noelle and Sarah.

I'd like to extend a thanks to the Cystic Fibrosis Trust and the MND Association for the information they've supplied and all the work they do. My stories often deal with matters that touch people in real life so please do check out their websites if you'd like more information.

Alongside them, as always, I'd like to thank my husband, Ben, my daughters, my mum and the dog! I'd also like to thank the Thomson clan for their support, and Sue Fortin, the Romaniacs, and Angela Marsons for being excellent writing buddies and also a tad crackers, the reason we're friends!

Last, I'd like to thank you. For reading this novel and getting this far. Books are just words until they are read and I'm so thankful for all my readers. A special thanks to those who've read one of my books and decided to read more. It's one of the best feelings as a writer to know that a story has been enjoyed enough to want to read more. If you've loved this book, do check out the rest and tell your friends. I'll be forever thankful!

PUBLISHING TEAM

Turning a manuscript into a book requires the efforts of many people. The publishing team at Bookouture would like to acknowledge everyone who contributed to this publication.

Commercial
Lauren Morrissette
Hannah Richmond
Imogen Allport

Cover design
Lisa Brewster

Data and analysis
Mark Alder
Mohamed Bussuri

Editorial
Jess Whitlum-Cooper
Imogen Allport

Copyeditor
Jane Eastgate

Proofreader
Becca Allen

Printed in Great Britain
by Amazon

49326796R00142